He grabbed up t[...] he demanded.

'Gideon.' Madison spoke in that gentle American drawl. 'I—I've signed the contract and will have it brought over to you,' she said.

Gideon was stunned. Madison had been upset about the contract earlier, and now she called and told him she'd signed the damned thing, without a single change!

'I can read your thoughts, Gideon,' Madison murmured in a wryly amused voice.

'I doubt it,' he drawled ruefully.

'I— Uncle Edgar had no right to interfere; I'm quite capable of fighting my own battles,' she said hardly.

Gideon smiled to himself. Now he *did* know the reason why Madison had signed the contract: stubborn pride. Well, he had enough of that himself, so maybe he did understand her, after all...

But not too much! After all, he had behaved out of character earlier when he'd kissed her. And now she had signed the contract the two of them were going to be constantly together for the next eight months at least...

Carole Mortimer says 'I was born in England, the youngest of three children—I have two older brothers. I started writing in 1978, and have now written over 100 books for Mills & Boon®.

'I have four sons—Matthew, Joshua, Timothy and Peter—and a bearded collie dog called Merlyn. I'm in a very happy relationship with Peter senior; we're best friends as well as lovers, which is probably the best recipe for a successful relationship. We live on the Isle of Man.'

Recent titles by the same author:

A MAN TO MARRY
A YULETIDE SEDUCTION
THEIR ENGAGEMENT IS ANNOUNCED

BOUND BY CONTRACT

BY
CAROLE MORTIMER

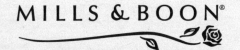

MILLS & BOON®

For Peter, my husband

DID YOU PURCHASE THIS BOOK WITHOUT A COVER?

If you did, you should be aware it is **stolen property** as it was reported *unsold and destroyed* by a retailer. Neither the author nor the publisher has received any payment for this book.

All the characters in this book have no existence outside the imagination of the author, and have no relation whatsoever to anyone bearing the same name or names. They are not even distantly inspired by any individual known or unknown to the author, and all the incidents are pure invention.

All Rights Reserved including the right of reproduction in whole or in part in any form. This edition is published by arrangement with Harlequin Enterprises II B.V. The text of this publication or any part thereof may not be reproduced or transmitted in any form or by any means, electronic or mechanical, including photocopying, recording, storage in an information retrieval system, or otherwise, without the written permission of the publisher.

This book is sold subject to the condition that it shall not, by way of trade or otherwise, be lent, resold, hired out or otherwise circulated without the prior consent of the publisher in any form of binding or cover other than that in which it is published and without a similar condition including this condition being imposed on the subsequent purchaser.

MILLS & BOON and MILLS & BOON with the Rose Device are registered trademarks of the publisher.

First published in Great Britain 2000
Harlequin Mills & Boon Limited,
Eton House, 18-24 Paradise Road, Richmond, Surrey TW9 1SR

© Carole Mortimer 2000

ISBN 0 263 81989 2

Set in Times Roman 10½ on 11½ pt.
01-0006-53144

Printed and bound in Spain
by Litografia Rosés, S.A., Barcelona

PROLOGUE

'I DON'T care what you thought, Edgar—I'm not interested in taking on one of your women!'

Edgar drew in a sharply angry breath. Gideon hadn't even let him finish saying what he wanted to say before jumping down his throat—something that just didn't happen to Edgar. As the owner of a production company, Edgar didn't often come up against opposition, and certainly not in this bluntly verbal way. But then, when had Gideon ever been anything else? It was just as well he thought of Gideon almost as his son, otherwise the younger man would now be feeling the brunt of his own anger.

Edgar had invited Gideon to this weekend party at his country home with the sole intention of introducing him to Madison. Unfortunately, Gideon had told him a short time ago that he would be leaving early in the morning, and Madison wasn't due to arrive until mid-afternoon, meaning that Edgar had to talk to him about Madison now...

And so, instead of giving the younger man the short, sharp reply he wanted to give, he gave him a look of intense irritation. 'Madison is not one of my women, damn it—she's my god-daughter!'

'That makes a change from nieces!' the younger man scorned. 'And considering you're an only child it's amazing where they keep appearing from; two in the last six months, I believe!'

'I wasn't aware anyone was counting,' Edgar felt stung into replying; he was a bachelor, for goodness' sake, and if at sixty-two he still found women attractive and beddable, he didn't expect to have to answer to anyone for it! 'I will say this once again, Gideon—and I'll emphasise this only once,' he added harshly; he might be very fond of Gideon, but the younger man's derision was unacceptable. 'Madison is the daughter of—an old friend of mine. She also happens to be an actress.'

Gideon, as a director, was in the process of casting his next film, and Edgar, as the head of the production company that Gideon was currently working for, had someone in mind for the lead of that film. Unfortunately, as Gideon himself was too aware, he was the director of the moment. He had walked off with the Best Director award at the Oscars the previous year, and it had been a feather in Edgar's cap that he'd managed to persuade Gideon to come back to England and work for his production company. But Gideon's own superior position almost meant Edgar didn't have the sway he would usually have with most other directors...

Gideon's mouth tightened. 'And I have never used the casting-couch approach when casting my films—and I'm not about to start now! Not even second-hand,' he added pointedly.

Edgar had to try very hard to hold on to his temper this time. Gideon was a good twenty years younger than him, and physically fitter than Edgar had been for some years— but, even so, Edgar could feel his own temper rising to the pitch of violence. 'I merely asked that you stay on until tomorrow afternoon so that you can meet Madison,' he said icily. 'I said nothing about going to bed with her!'

Gideon's mouth twisted mockingly. 'That's as well—I prefer to pick my own bed-partners!'

Edgar sighed. 'I think we're straying from the point here.'

'Not at all,' the younger man dismissed. 'You assured me I had a free hand with this film. Hell, you almost begged me to work for your production company—'

'I think "beg" is exaggerating things rather, Gideon,' he cut in dryly.

'Sorry,' Gideon returned without a tinge of regret in his voice, his mouth twisted with distaste. 'You probably prefer to save that for your nieces. Or god-daughters!' he added coldly.

Edgar didn't doubt that the young man was angry, and he was fond of Gideon—but even so…! 'I think you're going too far, Gideon,' he challenged. 'We go back a long way ourselves, and of course your father and I remained friends even after—'

'I don't ever recall using any of my family connections with you when we agreed that I'd work for your company,' Gideon cut in harshly, having stiffened defensively. 'So why don't we just agree not to discuss my father—or your god-daughter—for the rest of my stay here? Which ends in the morning,' he added pointedly.

Once again Edgar drew in a sharply angry breath. He'd certainly hit upon a raw nerve by mentioning Gideon's father. He would have been wiser not to have mentioned John—and definitely not to have almost mentioned the scandal that had ruined his career. He'd made a tactical error; Gideon's anger was not what he wanted at the moment. What he really wanted was for Gideon to stay here until tomorrow afternoon and meet Madison…!

For that reason Edgar again swallowed his own anger, visibly relaxing. 'I can assure you that Madison is not what you think she is,' he told the younger man smoothly. 'She's very talented—'

'What's her full name?'

'Madison McGuire.'

'Never heard of her,' Gideon dismissed scathingly, glancing around at the twenty or so other guests at Edgar's home for the weekend, obviously bored by their own conversation.

Edgar noticed that Gideon was distracted—and it angered him again. 'And you're never likely to if you won't even meet her!' he snapped. 'You want an unknown to play Rosemary; you said so yourself.'

'But it will be an unknown of my own choosing, not yours!' Gideon rasped, his grey eyes glacial as he met Edgar's gaze. 'Does she know about all this?' he scorned. 'Is that why you're pushing so hard? Does she think the part is already hers?' His mouth twisted scathingly.

He had pushed enough for the moment, Edgar realised; if he pushed any more just now Gideon might leave before he produced his pièce de résistance!

'Madison knows nothing about this conversation, Gideon,' he assured him smoothly; Madison would be no more pleased than Gideon if she did! 'Why don't we just forget about this for now—?'

'Let's just forget it—period, Edgar,' the other man drawled in a bored voice.

Edgar had no intention of doing any such thing. He was doing the right thing by introducing Madison to Gideon; he was sure of it. He just hoped that Susan, darling Susan, would forgive him when she found out what he had done! Susan...

'It's time to watch my private showing of the new Tony Lawrence film,' he told the younger man after receiving the signal from his manservant. 'I'm sure you're going to love it.' He wasn't sure of any such thing, but he was hoping— oh, yes, he was hoping...

But Gideon's expression, as he sat beside him before the lights went down in the private theatre in the basement of the house, didn't augur well. And so much depended on the next few minutes, so much more than even Gideon could guess. Otherwise he would already have walked out...!

Edgar kept his eyes on the screen, but he was completely

aware of the man sitting next to him. He knew exactly the moment Madison appeared, could feel Gideon's sudden tension, the way he sat forward in his seat, that habitual air of boredom that could be so irritating totally dissipated as his gaze was now riveted to the screen.

Yes!

Edgar could barely contain his own excitement. He was certain Gideon had taken the hook. Now all it depended on was whether or not they could get him to take the bait…!

One thing he did know: Gideon would not be leaving here early tomorrow morning, after all…

CHAPTER ONE

'I NEVER believed in mermaids until this moment!'

She didn't even open her eyes. The man with the silkily smooth voice was sure to be one of her uncle's guests, and from the little she had seen of *them* since her arrival he wouldn't be worth opening her eyes for!

She'd flown in from America only this afternoon; she was tired, jet-lagged, and desperate for sleep—which had proved impossible; her uncle had a houseful of guests for the weekend—noisy guests who seemed to invade most of the house.

She'd finally taken refuge in the swimming pool that took up half the basement of the house. Drifting on an air-bed, she felt the warmth of the water relaxing her in a way that couldn't be found in the main part of the house. The last thing she needed—or wanted—was to be found by one of her uncle's guests!

'No fish-tail,' she murmured disparagingly as she wriggled her toes pointedly, still half asleep, her hands trailing in the warmth of the water. Her body looked youthfully slender in a turquoise-coloured bikini, while her long blonde hair trailed in the water behind her.

'Mermaids don't have fish-tails when on land,' the man murmured mockingly.

'But I'm in the water,' she answered impatiently, keeping her face averted from the direction of his voice, wishing she'd never entered into the verbal exchange; perhaps if she had kept quiet he would have just gone away!

'*On* the water,' the man corrected her smoothly. 'Tell

me, is that accent for real, or are you just rehearsing for a part?' he added derisively.

Her mouth tightened. She wanted some peace and quiet; surely the fact that she was down here alone made that more than obvious? And yet this man persisted in talking to her, even passing comment on her American accent. In fact, he was a damned nuisance!

'Is *that* accent for real?' she returned in a perfect imitation of his educated English accent. 'Or are *you* just rehearsing for a part?'

'*Touché,*' he murmured appreciatively.

'What makes you think I'm an actress?' She felt drawn into asking, becoming intrigued in spite of herself.

'Most, if not all, of Edgar's guests this weekend are involved in the acting world,' the man drawled.

'Including yourself?' she prompted lightly.

'Including myself,' he confirmed dryly.

She wasn't impressed. Her mother had been full of dire warnings when she'd told her she wanted to be an actress, but one piece of her mother's advice she had learnt to take to heart: never become involved with anyone else in the business!

It was something she had to admit she'd learnt the hard way, falling for one of the male leads in the first play she'd ever been in off-Broadway. What she hadn't realised at the time was that his interest would last only as long as the run of the play—all of three weeks!—when he would then move on to the next play, the next gullible actress. She was still smarting from the experience. Of the man. And the folded play.

Which was why she'd taken one look at the guests here today and disappeared to the peace of the indoor swimming-pool; she could spend some time with Edgar once the other guests had gone. She still felt too emotionally raw to mix with the 'beautiful people' just yet!

She certainly hadn't expected to have her privacy invaded in this way. But then, the man had said he was involved in acting, so he was sure to be full of—

God, she was still angry at Gerry for turning out to be every inch the bastard her mother had warned her that actors could be! She'd thought she was over it, but obviously not...

Perhaps it was time she took a look at this mystery man. Who knew? He might just be the answer to every woman's prayer! Hell, she was becoming cynical on top of everything else!

'Everything else' was her disastrous love-affair with Gerry, and the fact that she was temporarily 'resting'. That sounded so interesting, but all it really meant was that she was out of work—again. All she had to show for her time at drama school was one walk-on part in a film, and a play that had folded after only three weeks; she 'rested' more than she worked!

'I shouldn't fall asleep in there, if I were you,' the man said mockingly, infuriatingly interrupting her solitude once again, letting her know that he hadn't gone away, as she'd hoped he might.

'Look, I thank you for your advice,' she snapped sarcastically, 'but I'll do what the hell I—' Her angry retort died on her lips as she finally turned her head to look at her tormenter. No! It couldn't be! This man was—'You—! I—!' Her shocked surprise was lost in a gurgle of water as, having now turned fully sideways to look at him, she totally lost her balance, falling into the water with a splash and a tangle of graceful limbs.

That man!

She knew him!

No, she didn't *know* him! She just—

God, this water tasted awful. And she seemed to be swallowing most of the pool. It was—

She had to get to the surface. She was slowly sinking to the bottom, and—

Suddenly there was a movement of water beside her, the strength of an arm about her waist, and she was being pulled roughly to the surface.

She would have started to swim to the side then, but that arm remained about her like a steel band, turning her over on to her back as she was pulled over to the side of the pool, before being dumped unceremoniously on to the side.

Even as she opened her mouth to protest at this man's rough handling of her she felt herself being rolled over on to her stomach, hands pounding against her back.

'Stop it!' she finally gasped, fighting for breath, her hands flying backwards as she tried to stop that painful pummelling. 'You're hurting me!' she cried impotently.

'Hurting you!' he repeated harshly, turning her over on to her back, a knee at either side of her body as he straddled her, cold water dripping over her from his wet clothes. 'I'd like to tan your backside!' His face was contorted with anger. 'Are you totally stupid, going into a pool alone when you can't even swim? I take back what I said about the mermaid; you looked like a stranded whale just now!'

She opened her mouth to protest at this verbal attack, and then closed it again. This man looked ready to carry out his threat to smack her!

Which wasn't surprising, when he'd obviously jumped into the water fully clothed in order to save her...!

No, she mustn't laugh—or she had no doubt he would tan her backside! This wasn't the time to see the funny side of this. That would have to come later!

'How gracious of you,' she drawled. 'But, contrary to what you may think, I can swim—very well, as it happens.' She had just been so surprised by the identity of this man that she'd forgotten to swim.

Gideon Byrne. Oscar-winning film director. She'd

watched the awards on television herself the previous year, seen him as he'd gone up on to the stage to collect his award, heard his brief acceptance speech. Tall and dark, with metallic-grey eyes, he had a presence that would have been electric on stage or film, but he'd chosen to use his talent behind rather than in front of the camera, and was as far removed from her in the world of acting as the sun was from the moon—and she had been treating him as nothing more than an irritating intrusion!

'Then I can only assume that on this occasion you lost your sense of direction—because you were heading for the bottom of the pool, not the top!' he scorned disgustedly, finally moving off her to sit down at the side of the pool, pushing an agitated hand through the dark wetness of his hair.

She became aware of her own dishevelled appearance, her hair a blonde tangle about her shoulders and down her back, her bikini affording her little cover. But then, she hadn't expected to see anyone. Or for anyone to see her!

She stood up in one fluid movement, moving to the lounger where she'd left her robe when she'd come down earlier. Pulling it on, she instantly felt warmer, and better able to deal with the situation.

'I really am sorry, Mr Byrne,' she began apologetically. 'I—'

'You know who I am?' he snapped harshly as he turned to look at her with coldly accusing eyes.

'Of course,' she acknowledged smoothly. 'Doesn't everyone?' she added lightly as he continued to glare at her.

She would have been decidedly out of touch in the acting world if she hadn't recognised this man. After his success the previous year the newspapers had been full of photographs and articles about him. Admittedly he was usually scowling in those photographs, but—

Not so different from now, really, she realised ruefully. She'd thought at the time that he probably didn't like having his photograph taken, that he was one of those directors who believed it was his work that was important, not his private life. But maybe it was just that he rarely smiled, after all…

'Not that I'm aware,' he dismissed coldly, standing up, giving her the full benefit of just how wet he actually was.

He was wearing black denims and a pale grey shirt— silk, if she weren't mistaken—and both articles of clothing were clinging to him. And, while the wetness of that clothing revealed just how masculine he was, his shoulders wide and powerful, his stomach flat, his hips tapered, he must also be very uncomfortable. And all because he'd thought she was drowning!

'You underestimate your fame, Mr Byrne,' she answered lightly. 'And I think perhaps you should get out of those wet clothes,' she suggested, with a guilty grimace. 'Before you catch pneumonia!'

'Not very likely in this hot-house.' But be began to unbutton his shirt anyway, revealing the dark hair that grew on his wide chest as he pulled the clinging material away from him and threw the dripping shirt down on to the tiled floor, before unbuttoning his denims, obviously with the intention of doing the same thing with them.

Much to her dismay! She might be twenty-two, and not a complete innocent where men were concerned, but she didn't usually have complete strangers stripping off in front of her, either!

'Er—I think Uncle Edgar left one of his robes in the changing room.' She turned away awkwardly. 'I'll go and check for you.' She moved hastily away, her cheeks hot with embarrassment, as Gideon Byrne continued to strip off his denims. Admittedly, he was wearing black briefs underneath, but there was no guarantee he wasn't going to strip those off next…!

Gideon Byrne, she thought breathlessly as she hurried to the changing room, trying to remember exactly what it was she had read about him in the newspapers the previous year. Thirty-eight, dark brown hair, grey eyes, unmarried, only child of the long-dead actor John Byrne…

But none of those cold facts could have prepared her for the flesh-and-blood man. How could the newspapers possibly describe the aura of electric energy that surrounded the man, or the cynicism that coloured every word he spoke? They couldn't. They *hadn't*!

Well, at least she had found the perfect cure for jet-lag; one dose of Gideon Byrne, and all the tiredness from her journey had completely left her!

Uncle Edgar hadn't mentioned that he had such a famous guest staying here when he'd met her at the airport earlier, or since her arrival at the house. If he had done, she might have been more prepared!

However, she was no more prepared for the sheer physical male beauty of his body when she returned with the robe—although, thankfully, he had kept the black briefs on!

She guessed he was well over six feet in height—as he seemed to tower over her five feet eight inches. His muscular body was deeply tanned; muscles rippled powerfully beneath his skin, and there was a fine sprinkling of dark hair over all of his body, becoming much thicker on the width of his chest. He was gorgeous!

'Thanks.'

She stared at him blankly for several seconds, wondering if she had spoken those words out loud, realising she hadn't as he held his hand out for the robe she carried.

'Sorry,' she muttered awkwardly, thrusting her hands into the pockets of her own towelling robe once he'd taken the one she was holding to pull on over his near-nakedness.

'*Uncle* Edgar?' He quirked dark brows at her questioningly as he tied the belt in place.

'It's an honorary title.' She was relieved to talk of something normal after the impact this man had made on her senses, hoping she wasn't making too big an idiot of herself. Although she thought she probably was! 'My name is Madison McGuire,' she told him lightly, holding out her hand. 'Edgar Remington is my godfather.'

Gideon Byrne didn't look impressed by this explanation; his mouth twisted scornfully as he touched her hand only lightly in return. Although it was enough for Madison to feel the thrill of electricity that ran up her arm. That aura didn't just surround him, it went right through him!

'Edgar is many things, to many people, but this is the first time I've heard him referred to as The Godfather!' he drawled.

Madison gave him a look of amused reproval. 'I doubt he would be flattered by that name!'

'Probably not,' Gideon Byrne accepted dryly. 'But he's a first-class manipulator nonetheless!'

She had known Edgar Remington all of her life. She knew him as a good friend of her parents, and also as her benevolent godfather, but she was aware there had to be another side to him, the side that headed one of the top film production companies in the world, and headed it well.

As a film director, perhaps that was the side of him that Gideon Byrne knew best...?

'I wouldn't know about that,' Madison dismissed with a shrug; her very minor part in a film might have been in one produced by Edgar's company, but even so she had had no contact with her uncle because of it, her almost non-existent role having been filmed on location in Scotland.

But what she did know was that dinner was going to be in an hour, and her hair was drying into tangles; she needed a shower and to wash her hair before the meal. She had half excused herself from attending dinner to Edgar earlier, saying she was too tired to be very good company for anyone, but after meeting this man she was wide awake. And hungry, she inwardly acknowledged.

'Wouldn't you?'

She gave Gideon a startled look, as much for the coldness of his tone as for the question itself. Was it her imagination, or was there an accusing edge to his voice? And, if so, what possible reason could this man have for feeling that way?

She gave a puzzled frown, shaking her head. 'It's getting late, Mr Byrne—'

'Call me Gideon,' he rasped harshly.

This man might be one of the most handsome men she'd ever set eyes on, but his manners certainly left a lot to be desired! And she'd always been led to believe Englishmen had the best manners in the world; obviously no one had acquainted Gideon Byrne with that fact!

She gave an acknowledging inclination of her head. 'It was very kind of you to jump into the water to save me earlier.'

'When you've known me a little longer—Madison, you'll realise kindness is not part of my nature!' he retorted harshly.

No, she didn't think it would be; he came over as a hard, unyielding man, one who rarely smiled. And she very much doubted she would get to know him 'a little longer'; their paths would never cross again after this weekend.

'Besides,' he added derisively, 'according to you, you didn't need saving!'

No, she hadn't, but it had still been kind of him to jump into the pool fully clothed, no matter what he might say to the contrary. 'If there's any permanent damage to your clothes, please do let me know,' she told him evenly. 'I'll be happy to replace them.' She wasn't quite sure how a silk shirt would stand up to the chemicals in the pool water!

'Oh, don't worry, you'll hear from me if that's the case,' he rasped. 'Tell me, is that the natural colour of your hair?'

'What…?' Madison was stunned by the abrupt change of subject—and the fact that the question didn't just border on being rude; it *was* rude!

At the moment, her hair was the colour of dark honey, but once she had washed and dried it it would be the colour of ripe corn, long and straight almost down to her waist. And, yes, it was her natural colour. As was the green of her eyes. And the light golden tan of her skin. In fact, all of her was real!

'You never can tell nowadays,' Gideon Byrne added insultingly, making no apology for the very personal remark.

'It's natural,' she answered him hardly, a perplexed frown marring her brow.

If she hadn't known better, she would have said this man disliked her. But surely that couldn't be so—the man didn't even know her. Probably he was just annoyed with her because of his unnecessarily wet clothing?

He nodded abruptly. 'I thought so.'

And…? But maybe there wasn't an 'and' with this man. He might be one of the top film directors in the world, with an Oscar at home to prove it, but he was also one of the coldest, rudest men Madison had ever met…

And, thinking of cold, she was starting to shiver now, and was badly in need of that hot shower she'd promised herself a few minutes ago. 'If you don't mind, I think I would like to go upstairs and take a shower before dinner,' she told him pleasantly.

He met her gaze challengingly. 'And if I do mind?' he drawled.

Madison didn't so much as blink at his rudeness this time. 'Then I'm still going upstairs to take a shower,' she said bluntly. Maybe that was the only way to be with this man; politeness certainly didn't seem to work!

To her surprise, he smiled. And it transformed his face from austere coldness to friendly warmth. Well…almost, she decided. Friendly was perhaps going too far! But he did look more approachable, Madison tried to convince herself. Not that she intended 'approaching' him; she was quite happy to just part on that one smile, sure that it was more than a lot of people got out of him.

'Maybe you and I are going to get on after all, Madison McGuire,' he murmured enigmatically.

She wasn't sure she would go quite that far on the basis of one smile! Besides, there must be mere hours left of his visit—hardly long enough for them to need to 'get on'…

'If you say so,' she acknowledged noncommittally. 'Nice to have met you, Mr Byrne,' she added politely before turning to leave.

'Liar!' came his softly taunting reply from behind her.

Madison paused, turning slowly back to face him. 'I'm not in the habit of lying, Mr Byrne—'

'I thought I told you to call me Gideon,' he rasped harshly.

She frowned. 'Perhaps you did—Mr Byrne,' she felt stung into replying; really, the man was nothing but an arrogant bully! 'But—'

'We haven't been formally introduced?' he cut in derisively. 'I think it's a little late in our acquaintance for that; after all, I did attempt to save your life a short time ago!'

'Attempt' just about described it! If he hadn't startled her in the way he had, she wouldn't have fallen into the water in the first place!

'I was about to say—but I really couldn't be so familiar with a film director of your calibre,' she finished forcefully. 'But on second thoughts…! I'm not in the habit of lying— Gideon, and it hasn't been nice meeting you at all!' She turned on her heel and walked away, going up the stairs that led back to the main part of the house.

And, as she did so, she could swear she heard the sound of Gideon Byrne chuckling down in the pool-room.

Ridiculous. That man didn't even know *how* to chuckle!

What a monumental pain in the—! She had never met anyone like him. Cold. Rude. Arrogant. If that was what being awarded an Oscar did for you, she hoped she never got one!

Not that she was ever likely to, she groaned inwardly, if she went around upsetting directors of Gideon Byrne's calibre.

Oh, hell!

Best just to forget she had ever met him. With any luck, he would have left before dinner…

Gideon's humour faded as soon as he heard the loud thud of the door closing behind her.

She had pluck; he would give her that. She was also incredibly beautiful, in exactly the way he had noticed on the screen last night as he'd sat watching the Tony Lawrence film.

He had immense respect for the other director, and as he hadn't had the chance to see his new film yet he'd enjoyed watching it from a technical angle, anyway. But when the serving girl had walked across the screen it was as if he had been given an electric shock…!

He'd been looking for just such a girl for the last six months, seen dozens of would-be-hopefuls, but none of them were exactly what he wanted. When Madison McGuire had walked across the screen last night he'd known he had at last seen his Rosemary.

She was everything he wanted Rosemary to be: the delicately beautiful face of an angel, the deep green of her eyes as she looked briefly at the camera a bonus he hadn't been expecting, her neck long and creamy, looking too fragile to support the weight of that long, corn-coloured hair, her body boyishly slender, her legs, he had discovered only minutes ago, long and coltish.

Yes, she was everything he was looking for, and as he'd avidly studied the credits, looking for her name, he had read 'Madison McGuire' next to 'serving girl'.

Madison McGuire! The very girl Edgar had been trying minutes ago to persuade him to stay on and meet. And as he'd glanced sideways at Edgar he'd seen that smile of satisfaction on the older man's face. Damn him!

Part of Gideon had wanted to say to hell with Edgar and this Madison, and just leave as he'd planned. But the other part of him, the purely professional part, had known he would be a fool if he left without even seeing her. Although it had gone against the grain to tell Edgar he had decided to stay on another day after all. Especially as Edgar had taken his decision so calmly, only the twinkling blue of his eyes giving away the fact that he was well aware of exactly what—and who!—had changed Gideon's mind!

Well, now he had seen Madison.

And she was everything, if not more than he had been looking for in the lead for his next film. The American accent had come as a bit of a surprise; Edgar had forgotten to mention that little fact when he'd spoken of her, and in her part in last night's film she had merely murmured 'Thank you, sir'—which had given him no idea where she came from. But she had proved minutes ago that she was perfectly capable of adopting an English accent if she needed to—if only to mock him with!

Yes, he had seen Madison McGuire. Now all he had to do was offer her the part of Rosemary. It was whether or not she would accept that he wasn't altogether sure of. She would be a fool if she didn't; the film would be the making of her career. It all depended on just how much she'd decided it hadn't been nice meeting him!

'Been for a swim, Gideon?'

Edgar! Just his luck to walk straight into his host in the hallway, Gideon decided as he slowly turned.

Or was it luck? Edgar looked confidently amused—as if he was well aware under what circumstances Gideon had been for a 'swim'. Perhaps his 'goddaughter' had run to Uncle Edgar with the tale of the terrible Gideon Byrne?

Or maybe not. Madison, for all she looked so fragile, had been perfectly capable of fighting her own battles a few minutes ago—at least, verbally!

'I met Madison down at the pool,' he told the other man dryly.

'Yes?' Edgar returned confidently.

It was that confidence that rankled so much with Gideon. It bordered on smug—and it made Gideon want to wipe the smile right off Edgar's face!

He shrugged. 'I didn't have a costume, but that didn't seem to bother Madison too much,' he told the other man challengingly.

Edgar's humour faded, his eyes taking on that steely quality that would be a warning to lesser men than Gideon. 'I sincerely hope you're joking, Gideon,' he bit out tersely. 'Madison is here for a little TLC, not to deal with idiots who choose to go skinny-dipping in my pool!'

Gideon could tell that Edgar was more than a little annoyed; he would never have called him an idiot otherwise. But it was his reference to Madison needing TLC that intrigued him. Madison had looked no more than twenty or so, hardly old enough to be recovering from a broken marriage or something like that. Which begged the question, what could be the reason she needed TLC? But it wasn't a question he intended asking Edgar—he wouldn't give the other man the satisfaction!

He shrugged, smiling grimly. 'I told you, Madison didn't seem to mind. Now, if you'll excuse me,' he added as Edgar seemed intent on pursuing the subject, 'I think I'll follow her example and take a shower before dinner.'

Edgar's eyes were narrowed to steely slits. 'I thought you were leaving before dinner?'

Last night he had decided he would take a look at this Madison McGuire and then leave, and he had told Edgar the latter, at least. But now that he had seen Madison there was no way he was leaving here until he had spoken to her, and looked at her, some more. There was a hell of a lot of work to do, and he didn't have too much time left in which to do it. In fact, now that he had seen Madison, there was no time to lose.

He shrugged again. 'I changed my mind. See you later, Edgar,' he told the other man firmly before walking away.

Edgar had brought Madison to his attention, and that was the end of the other man's involvement in the situation as far as Gideon was concerned. He didn't give a damn what she was to the other man; if she was going to work for Gideon, she was going to do it on his terms.

Or not at all!

CHAPTER TWO

'WELL, well, well, if it isn't Madison McGuire; I wondered if I would recognise you with your clothes on!'

Madison had tensed at the first sound of Gideon Byrne's infuriating voice, but at his last remark she spun round indignantly. What did he think he was doing?

She had been relieved earlier when she'd entered the sitting-room for a pre-dinner drink to discover that Gideon Byrne wasn't there, breathing easier when she realised she wouldn't be having another verbal fencing match with him all evening.

She'd even relaxed enough to indulge in a mild flirtation with Drew Armitage, a man she knew slightly from working on the film in Scotland some months before. Drew was boyishly handsome, and she'd easily been able to see his admiration for her, dressed in the figure-hugging flame-coloured dress, her hair newly washed, cascading in loose golden curls down her back, her subtle make-up highlighting the deep green of her eyes.

A quick glance at Drew now, after Gideon's deliberately provocative remark, and she knew he was adding two and two together and coming up with five!

'Gideon!' she greeted smoothly, moving to kiss him warmly on the cheek. 'You dress up real nice yourself,' she told him in a husky Southern drawl.

He did dress up nice, she inwardly acknowledged, the black dinner suit and snowy white shirt tailored to his muscular frame, his handsome face appearing as if etched from stone, although there was a mocking glint in the dark grey of his eyes as he returned her gaze. He was enjoying himself, Madison realised...

'Do you know Drew?' She turned pointedly to the other man. 'Drew, this is—'

'Gideon Byrne,' the younger man finished, a slightly awed expression on his face as he shook hands with him. 'I enjoyed *Shifting Time* very much.' He referred to Gideon's Oscar-winning film.

'Thanks,' Gideon said smoothly. 'I thought you were rather good in *Hidden Highland*.'

Drew looked suitably pleased by the praise; it was Madison who looked at Gideon through narrowed lids. *Hidden Highland* was her only film credit to date, her entire part comprising all of two lines, both of them mundane. But Gideon had seen the film. Had he noticed her in it too...?

Gideon returned her gaze with raised brows. 'Something wrong, Madison?' he prompted mockingly.

Even if he had recognised her in the film, Madison realised he wasn't about to comment on her performance! Not that there had been much to comment on. He might even have gone out to the bathroom during the three-minute section of the film that she had appeared in!

'Not in the least, Gideon,' she returned lightly. 'Don't let us keep you, if you would like to go and help yourself to a drink,' she added dismissively.

Gideon's mouth twisted ruefully as he held back a smile, obviously easily able to see her words for what they were—and to be amused by them!

'I was just about to go and get myself a refill,' Drew put in quickly. 'Could I get something for you while I'm there?' He looked enquiringly at the older man.

'An orange juice would be fine, thanks,' Gideon accepted, his gaze still fixed on Madison.

And it was a very unnerving gaze, Madison decided. It had been bad enough down at the pool earlier, but now she felt as if the damned man was dissecting everything about her. There was certainly none of the admiration of her appearance in his dark grey gaze that she'd seen in Drew's!

'Madison?' Drew prompted softly.

'I'm fine, thanks.' She indicated her glass, still half full with white wine.

'You shouldn't drink too much of that stuff, you know,' Gideon bit out tersely once the other man had left to get the drinks.

'I shouldn't?' Madison eyed him warily—the trouble with this man, she decided, was you never quite knew what he was going to say next!

He shook his head. 'How old are you?'

Like that! What on earth did her age have to do with anything?

'Twenty-two,' she answered cautiously.

'Hmm.' Gideon pulled a face. 'Well, the alcohol obviously hasn't started having an effect on you yet. At least, outwardly—you only look about eighteen! But inwardly it may be a different matter.'

Madison frowned up at him. Somewhere in all of that she felt he had given her a compliment—it was just so ambiguous it didn't feel like one! 'You don't drink, Gideon?' She had noticed his request for only orange juice.

'No,' he returned harshly. 'It impedes rather than heightens the senses, has a disastrous effect on the skin and body organs, is—'

'I get the gist, Gideon,' she cut in laughingly; this was a house party, for goodness' sake, not an AA meeting! 'As it happens, I only drink wine, and then only on occasions like this.' She looked around them pointedly at the groups of other chattering guests.

He shrugged, no answering humour in his own stern expression. 'That's the way most people start. You—'

'Here we are.' Drew arrived back with the drinks, hand-ing the older man the requested orange juice. 'I hope you'll both excuse me.' He smiled apologetically. 'Edgar just wants to have a quick word with me.'

'Really?' Gideon returned mockingly.

'Hmm.' Drew nodded. 'Nice to meet you, Gideon. I'll catch up with you later, Madison.' He squeezed her arm lightly in parting.

She watched as Drew hurried over to where her uncle Edgar stood waiting for him near the window, Edgar giving an acknowledging inclination of his head in Madison and Gideon's direction before turning away to talk to Drew.

'I wonder what Edgar is finding to talk to him about?' Gideon mused dryly at her side. 'Whatever it is, I'm damned sure it wasn't important enough that Edgar had to talk to him right this moment! Except as a means of leaving the two of us alone together,' he added scathingly.

Madison turned slowly to look at him, frowning. 'What do you mean?'

He made it sound as if her godfather was matchmaking, and, as Edgar was fully aware of the raw state of her emotions, she couldn't see that being the case at all. In fact, when she'd seen Uncle Edgar earlier, and told him about the disaster down in the pool-room, he'd looked more than a little irritated. Until she made him see the funny side of it.

Although she still didn't find it that funny herself...

Gideon looked at her with mocking eyes. 'I told you earlier that Edgar is a manipulator,' he said enigmatically.

He might be, but he wasn't a sadist—and matching her with a cynic like Gideon Byrne would definitely put him in that category!

She shrugged. 'And, as I explained then, I just don't see him like that.' She looked around, wondering if there was anyone else she could go off and talk to. Anyone, as long as she didn't have to stand here talking to this man any longer!

But there was no one else that she knew in the room—several faces she recognised, of course, but not through personal knowledge, only from films or television. Edgar certainly knew some famous people; in fact, she was a little out of place in such distinguished company. Including the man at her side!

'I wouldn't bother, if I were you,' Gideon drawled as he watched her quick survey of the room. 'Edgar would veer anyone off who looked like interrupting us!'

She turned back to him, a frown once again marring her creamy brow. In fact, she had frowned so much since meeting this man earlier today, she was surprised he hadn't told her she shouldn't do that, either!

'Any why would he do that?' she prompted lightly.

Gideon shrugged. 'Because he wants to give me the time to offer you a screen-test with a view to a part in my next film. And for you to have the time to accept the offer!'

Madison stared at him. She seemed to do that a lot around this man too! But then he said some of the most outrageous—and unbelievable things. A screen-test! This man wanted to give her a screen-test? With a view to being in his next film—

No, that wasn't what he had said... What he had actually said was her *uncle Edgar* wanted him to do that, which wasn't the same thing at all!

She gave a rueful smile. 'You'll have to forgive Uncle Edgar.' She grimaced. 'He's just a very doting godfather, who means well, but doesn't see that—'

'He's a very powerful doting godfather,' Gideon put in harshly.

And it was obvious this man resented whatever power Edgar might have tried to exert over him on Madison's behalf. Which she couldn't exactly blame him for. Gideon

Byrne was a powerful man in his own right, and her god-father, if he had tried to force Madison into this man's notice, should have thought of that.

If he had. She wasn't absolutely sure that Gideon hadn't just misunderstood Edgar.

'I see it's time for us to go in to dinner,' Gideon drawled as the other guests began to stroll towards the dining-room.

Madison was still so inwardly disturbed by what Gideon had said about her godfather that she offered no protest when he took a firm hold of her arm and took her into the dining-room with him.

'You see?' Gideon murmured derisively when it turned out that Madison was seated between himself and Drew at the long oak table.

She was starting to! But Edgar, when she looked down the long table to where he sat at its head, appeared to be so engrossed in what the lady to his right was saying to him that he didn't seem aware of Madison's compelling gaze levelled at him.

'So when can you come in for a screen-test?'

She turned to give Gideon a startled look—a look he returned with cold, unblinking grey eyes. 'You can't be serious!' she finally managed to gasp.

'I'm never anything else where my work is concerned,' he informed her grimly. 'I saw you in *Hidden Highland*,' he admitted dryly. 'You have a certain—look that I find…interesting,' he continued guardedly. 'I'll be able to tell you more once I've had you read for me, but…' He shrugged. 'Let's just wait and see, shall we?'

Wait and see!

Wait and see what? This man might be one of the hottest film directors in Hollywood at the moment—the public waiting with bated breath to see what his next film was going to be—but in the few hours Madison had known him she had also discovered that he was rude and arrogant, cynical to the point of being unbearable. Even if he should—by some miracle!—offer her a part in his film, how on earth would she ever be able to work with such a man?

Don't envisage situations that don't yet exist, she told herself firmly. And which may never exist, she added ruefully. She didn't believe Gideon liked her any more than she liked him.

'Eat your dinner,' he instructed abruptly; most of the other guests were already halfway through their starter of smoked salmon mousse.

She felt a resentful flush in her cheeks. 'I'm twenty-two, Gideon,' she snapped, 'not two!'

'*Please* eat your dinner?' He arched mocking brows.

It was certainly an improvement, but from him it still sounded like an order!

But Madison wasn't in the mood for any more conversation with him! 'Better,' she nodded, picking up her knife and fork and beginning to eat.

To her surprise she heard the chuckle she'd thought she'd heard earlier down in the pool-room, and so she looked up at Gideon with quizzical green eyes.

He looked younger when he laughed, less strained, even the grey of his eyes taking on a luminous quality. He also, in this more relaxed state, reminded her of someone—she just couldn't quite place who...

'What is it?' He sobered as she looked thoughtful.

She shook her head. 'Nothing.' It would come to her, but in the meantime she didn't intend discussing it with Gideon. 'You should smile more often, though; it makes you look half human!' She regretted her bluntness as soon as the words left her mouth; it was just that this man irritated her so much, all her own social niceties seemed to desert her in favour of his own rudeness whenever she was around him.

Her mother would have been horrified if she could hear

her. She'd always impressed upon her that good manners cost nothing, but that they invariably made a good impression. The trouble with that theory around Gideon Byrne was that he didn't seem to have a good impression of anyone, least of all her!

'Only half human, hmm?' He quirked mocking brows. 'What do you think the other half of me is?'

He wouldn't like it if she told him! 'Eat your dinner, Gideon.' She briskly repeated his own order.

He shook his head. 'You remind me of a teacher I had at school. The Dragon, we used to call her!'

Much more of this and she would tell him what *she* mentally called *him*—and it was nowhere near as polite as The Dragon!

'Did you go to school in England, Gideon?' She lightly changed the subject, putting her knife and fork neatly on the plate as she gave up all hope of eating the smoked salmon. Her appetite hadn't been that great once she realised Gideon was still here, anyway, but now that she was actually seated next to him…!

A shutter seemed to come down over his eyes, giving them that steely quality once again, while his mouth became a thin, straight line, his body no longer relaxed, but strained with tension.

She'd only asked if he'd gone to school in England, for goodness' sake; she had thought that would be a safe subject for them to talk about. Obviously she'd thought wrong!

'Why do you ask?' he rasped suspiciously.

'No reason,' she shrugged, wondering what she could have said wrong this time; talking to this man was like walking across a minefield! 'I was educated in the States, obviously, but, being an actor, your father probably worked mainly in America, so I just wondered—'

'My parents separated when I was seven,' Gideon put in

harshly. 'And I lived in England with my mother from that age, so yes, I was educated in England!'

His parents' separation had been *that* particular mine-field! Well, how was she supposed to know that? Gideon would already have been sixteen by the time she was born, and his father had been long dead before she'd become aware of his films.

John Byrne had been of the Steve McQueen, Dustin Hoffman era, but he had died young, in his thirties, having only made a dozen or so films before his death. Yet his brilliance on screen had been undoubted, his charisma electric.

But perhaps his parents' separation, and the subsequent death of his father, explained why Gideon was so remote himself? It was a sad fact of life that if you didn't love anyone, then you couldn't be hurt by their loss.

Maybe if Madison had appreciated that earlier she wouldn't have been so hurt by Gerry's defection!

Although she could never see herself being as emotionally removed as Gideon Byrne.

'What about your own family, Madison?' Gideon cut in on her thoughts. 'I'm interested in why it is you have an English godparent,' he added dryly as she looked at him questioningly.

He might be 'interested', but that was a curiosity Madison didn't intend satisfying. 'An English godparent who spends a lot of his time in the States,' she dismissed lightly. 'And yes, I have family: my mother and father, and an older brother. They all live in Nevada.'

'But not you,' Gideon said thoughtfully.

'Some of the time I do,' she corrected him; she spent quite a lot of time at home 'resting'! 'But an invitation from Edgar is hard to refuse!'

'So I've found,' he acknowledged grimly.

On further acquaintance with this man she didn't believe

he could ever be forced into doing something he didn't want to do; Edgar might have issued the invitation, but Gideon was here because he chose to be.

'Mm, this looks delicious!' She thankfully turned her attention to the main course that had now been placed in front of her. 'I just love English roast beef with all the trimmings!'

'Makes a change from burgers, hmm?' Gideon taunted.

She hadn't even tasted a burger until she was in her teens and out with her friends one evening. Her mother had always insisted on a healthy diet for her two children, with plenty of vegetables, chicken and fish, and after trying that one burger Madison had had to agree with her!

'A struggling actress has to eat what she can afford,' she returned noncommittally.

Gideon shrugged. 'Then it's just as well you stopped struggling.'

'I—' She abruptly stopped speaking as she realised exactly what he was implying. 'We're both guests in Edgar's home, Gideon,' she bit out angrily. 'I suggest we both try and act that way!'

How dared he even think—! *Who* did he think—? He was the most impossible, insulting man Madison had ever met!

And she for one wasn't going to waste any more of her time on him. She turned to her left to talk to Drew when she wasn't concentrating on her food, totally ignoring Gideon now—a fact he didn't seem particularly bothered by, chatting easily with the woman sitting on his right.

There had been no mistaking his implication concerning her relationship with Edgar; this man didn't believe for one minute that she was actually the other man's god-daughter!

Well, he was mistaken, because that was exactly what she was—*all* she was to Edgar. Oh, she knew about Edgar's reputation with women; her mother had been teasing him for years about the fact that it was time he settled down with just one woman. Edgar's usual reply to that was the only woman he would possibly be interested in marrying was already married to someone else. He meant her mother, of course…

But Edgar's reputation as a ladies' man did not give Gideon Byrne the right to jump to conclusions concerning Madison's relationship with him, and she deeply resented his implication that she was using Edgar to further her career. As far as she was concerned, Gideon could stick his screen-test—

'I think you've had enough, don't you?'

She turned sharply at the sound of Gideon's mocking voice, looking down at the wine glass in her hand. She had allowed her glass to be filled a couple of times during the meal, if only in an effort to show Gideon Byrne—who she was sure knew exactly how much wine she had drunk!—that she would do exactly what she wanted to do, and his opinion counted for nothing.

And it still counted for nothing!

Her green eyes flashed a warning as she met his derisive gaze. 'I think I'm perfectly capable of knowing for myself when I've had enough wine to drink—thank you,' she said hardly.

His mouth twisted. 'I wasn't referring to the wine,' he drawled. 'Although I agree you've probably had enough of that too—'

'You—'

'I was actually referring to the fact you look as if you're about to keel over into your coffee,' he continued dryly.

The fact that he was right irritated her anew. She was so tired now, she felt as if she was swaying on her seat, and, as Gideon had guessed, the feeling had nothing to do with the wine she had consumed! She'd been without sleep for almost forty-eight hours now, and the last six had, since meeting Gideon Byrne, been anything but restful!

'I think I'm also capable of deciding when it's time for me to go to bed,' she told him stubbornly.

'Are you?' His expression was deliberately bland.

Once again Madison felt that overwhelming urge to hit him! But at the same time a wave of such exhaustion swept over her, she didn't feel as if she had the strength to lift her hand...

'Time to go,' Gideon announced firmly, standing up to pull back her chair for her.

She looked up at him, unmoving, for several seconds and saw several other people looking in their direction. If she continued to just sit there, with Gideon pointedly waiting for her to stand up, *all* the other people at the table would eventually be staring at them!

Rather than have that happen, Madison stood up. At least, she attempted to. As she got to her feet her legs buckled beneath her, only Gideon's arm about her waist stopping her from actually falling to the carpeted floor.

He kept that arm about her waist as he guided her out of the dining-room. Which was just as well, because she was falling asleep on her feet now.

'You're very kind—'

'I told you, Madison,' Gideon cut in huskily, 'kindness isn't in my nature. I got you out of there before you made an idiot of yourself for one reason, and one reason only,' he added gratingly. 'When I introduce you to the world as the star of my next film, I don't want anyone remembering I had to carry you out of a room because you were drunk!'

But she wasn't drunk!

And what did he mean, the star of his next film? He didn't mean *her*! Did he...

Madison didn't get a chance to ask him that question;

exhaustion and the relaxing glasses of wine were finally taking their toll, and she fell asleep on Gideon's shoulder...

He'd got her out of the room just in time, Gideon acknowledged grimly as he swung her up into his arms and began to ascend the winding staircase. Another couple of minutes, and—

'What the hell do you think you're doing?'

Gideon glanced down to where Edgar stood in the large entrance hall, the older man scowling up at him darkly. 'What does it look like I'm doing?' he snapped impatiently.

'That's what I would like to know!' Edgar followed him up the staircase, looking down at the sleeping Madison cradled in Gideon's arms. 'What have you done to her?'

'Don't be ridiculous, Edgar,' he told the other man harshly. 'At a guess, I would say she's exhausted. And she weighs a lot more than she looks,' he muttered grimly, 'so tell me which bedroom is hers before I drop her!'

Gideon wasn't about to do any such thing; Madison was a mere featherweight, despite what he had said, but Edgar's accusing attitude was annoying him intensely. He was trying to help Madison avoid embarrassing herself, and Edgar was treating him as if he were about to ravish the unconscious woman!

'This way,' Edgar bit out coldly, leading the way down a hallway to a room right at the end.

'I should have known it would be the furthest away!' he rasped as Edgar pushed the door open for Gideon to precede him. Gideon laid Madison down gently on top of the bed before straightening to look at the older man. 'Shall I undress her, or will you?' he challenged provocatively.

An angry flush darkened Edgar's cheeks. 'I don't think Madison would appreciate either of us doing that!' He moved to cover her with the bedcovers.

Gideon found himself irritated by the tenderness with

which Edgar removed Madison's shoes, and tucked the cover under her chin and over her shoulders.

He had been impressed by the looks of the woman he had met down in the pool earlier, and even more impressed this evening when Madison continued to verbally fence with him. She'd even made him laugh a couple of times!

The way that Madison looked, the fragility of her, would be a perfect foil for the character of Rosemary. And the more he saw of Madison McGuire, the more convinced he became that she could play the part.

The main problem he had with that was Edgar. The other man had been so damned sure of himself last night when he'd spoken of Madison, so smug, that Gideon baulked at the idea of using someone Edgar had put forward.

But was that enough of a reason to reject, out of hand, the only real possibility he had seen for Rosemary in the last six months?

The answer to that had to be no!

He turned to look at Madison with narrowed eyes. She looked even younger when she was asleep, a baby innocence to her delicate features, her golden hair spread out on the pillow beneath her, the figure-hugging red dress that outlined her curves so lovingly, and so belied that youthful innocence, hidden from view under the bedspread.

And awake there was a fire in those amazing green eyes, a grit about her that refused to be cowed. By anybody. And Gideon had to admit he had given her a hard time this evening!

But she'd withstood it well, had given back as good as she got. Those were the inner qualities that needed to be brought to the character of Rosemary...

But he did not want Edgar, as the doting godfather, breathing down his neck when he worked!

'She's very beautiful, isn't she?'

He turned sharply to the older man. 'Very,' he rasped.

'And?' Edgar arched questioning brows.

Gideon gave a sigh. 'And nothing, Edgar. I see dozens of beautiful women every day; it doesn't mean they can act worth a damn!'

Edgar stiffened. 'Madison can act.'

He shrugged. 'So you keep telling me.'

'So you would know, if you would only—'

'I'm my own man, Edgar.' He cut in harshly on the other man's forcefulness. 'If you don't like it, then maybe you got yourself the wrong director!' He looked indignantly at the older man.

He could see anger warring with prudence inside Edgar as he tried to stop himself saying something he was going to regret. The fact that the older man did that at all was indicative of how much this meant to him.

Gideon glanced once again at the sleeping Madison. 'Who is she, Edgar?' He frowned heavily.

Was it his imagination, or did the older man look evasive, just for a brief moment? If he did, it was so fleeting it was barely there at all. But, even so, Gideon felt uneasy. There was something about his god-daughter Edgar wasn't telling him...

'You said she's the daughter of an old friend of yours...?' he prompted slowly.

'That's right,' Edgar answered briskly. 'Malcolm McGuire.'

Which meant precisely nothing to Gideon. Nevertheless, he still felt there was something Edgar was holding back...

'Should I know him?' he persisted.

Edgar shrugged. 'I doubt it. He's a businessman. Casinos,' he added as Gideon continued to look at him with narrowed eyes.

Which was why the family was based in Nevada, Gideon realised.

His gaze returned to Madison as she lay innocently sleeping. There was something here that didn't add up. He just didn't know what it was! And it was a sure fact Edgar wasn't going to be the one to tell him!

Gideon could feel it inside him; Madison McGuire was going to be trouble.

The question was, would she be worth that trouble...?

CHAPTER THREE

MADISON'S eyelids felt as if they were glued together, and even when she opened them the bright daylight seemed to hurt.

She lay on the bed looking at the window, totally disorientated, the curtains undrawn. Then she remembered— she was at Uncle Edgar's country home. And she must have been so tired last night she had forgotten to pull the curtains before falling asleep. As she looked slowly around the room, and finally down at herself, she realised she was still wearing the red dress from last night too.

She must have been very tired not to have even—

Gideon Byrne!

The name exploded inside her head like a bomb, making her wince with the impact, as did the memory of this man. He had annoyed and taunted her last night to the point where she'd ended up turning her back on him as she ate. The last thing she remembered was feeling so tired, she felt as if she was going to fall asleep on her chair—

No—that wasn't the last thing she remembered!

Gideon Byrne had helped her to her feet, his arm about her waist as he helped her from the dining-room. And— and—he had thought she was drunk!

Madison sat up abruptly as she remembered that accusation. She had drunk two or three glasses of wine, she accepted that, but—

She turned sharply as a brisk knock on the door preceded her uncle Edgar's entrance into the bedroom, a tray in his hand, smiling at her as he placed the latter down on the bed beside her. Madison looked down blankly at the toast and orange juice. Breakfast! Uncle Edgar had brought her breakfast—when she felt as if consuming either the toast or juice would choke her.

'It's only a light snack because lunch is in two hours,' he explained lightly as he sat on the end of her bed. 'Did you sleep well?'

How should she know? She didn't even remember falling asleep, let alone know if it had been restful! 'I think so,' she answered softly, eyeing him guardedly. Uncle Edgar didn't look annoyed or anything like that; in fact, he looked rather pleased with himself, so she couldn't have thoroughly disgraced herself last night. 'What time is it?' She took a sip of the orange juice, its sharpness not choking her as she had suspected but helping to wake her up.

Although if waking up meant she had to fence words with Gideon Byrne again she thought she would prefer to go back to sleep!

'It's eleven o'clock,' Uncle Edgar answered her ruefully. 'And don't look so worried, Madison; he's gone!' He chuckled as if at a great joke as her eyes widened guiltily, absently picking up a piece of the toast and biting into it hungrily.

She swallowed hard. 'I—'

'Don't try telling me you don't know who I'm talking about.' He shook his head in teasing reproval. 'Gideon left here at eight o'clock this morning. But he left this for you.' He held out an envelope.

Madison looked at it as the victim must look at the snake—just before the latter struck! What could Gideon Byrne possibly be writing to her about?

'It's his card.' Uncle Edgar continued to munch on his toast, putting the envelope down on the bed as Madison made no effort to take it from him. 'He wants you to ring him.'

She gasped. 'He wants me to—! I have no intention of calling him.' She gave a determined shake of her head.

If she never saw Gideon Byrne again it would be too soon. He might be a brilliant film director, but as a human being he was certainly wanting. And as a man—! As a man he exuded a lethal sensuality that was totally dispelled the moment he opened his cynical mouth! More than that, he made her feel uncomfortable. And she'd never thought of herself lacking in confidence until she'd encountered that man!

Edgar slowly put down his toast, his eyes narrowed now, his mouth unsmiling. 'Don't be an idiot, Madison,' he grated. 'Of course you're going to call him.'

She sighed, shaking her head. 'I dislike the man intensely,' she said with feeling.

'No one's asking you to sleep with him—'

'I should damn well hope not!' Madison protested, her green eyes wide with indignation.

'There's a saying about protesting too much—but I won't bore you with it at the moment,' Edgar added quickly as angry colour darkened her cheeks. 'If it makes you feel any better, Gideon assures me he isn't into the casting couch routine himself,' he added dismissively. 'So— What is it now?' He frowned as Madison muttered something.

'I was just wondering when the two of you had this insightful conversation,' she said incredulously, putting the tray down on the side table before getting up off the bed, glaring down disgustedly at her godfather.

'After dinner a couple of days ago, actually,' Edgar dismissed. 'Now, look, Madison, don't start being bull-headed with me about this. Gideon wants you to go in for a screen-test—'

'Did you find that out from the card in the envelope too?' she cut in accusingly. She didn't care what Gideon wanted; she wasn't here to be at his beck and call.

'Not exactly,' Edgar drawled.

'Something else the two of you discussed at this insightful conversation after dinner?' She was becoming so angry
she was shaking with it.

It sounded to her as if Uncle Edgar and Gideon Byrne
had discussed a hell of a lot more than Gideon's method
of casting his films, and on top of his remarks last night
about how powerful her uncle Edgar was she didn't particularly like the sound of that. In fact, she would be more
than a little unhappy if it should turn out her godfather had
been instrumental in Gideon Byrne's offering her this
screen-test…!

'Don't be difficult over this, Madison—'

'I'm never difficult, Uncle Edgar,' she cut in forcefully.
'But I'm not stupid, either,' she added heatedly. 'If you
have somehow used your influence to get Gideon Byrne to
offer me a screen-test—'

'You've met the man, Madison,' Edgar interrupted derisively. 'Did he strike you as someone who could be in-
fluenced?'

No, he hadn't… In fact, he'd said almost as much to her
last night. But she still didn't believe Edgar was completely
innocent in all of this; he looked far too self-satisfied for
that to be the case.

'It will probably be a waste of time, anyway,' she told
him crossly. 'Prestigious as being in a Gideon Byrne movie
would be, another one- or two-line part isn't exactly going
to make me a star—' She broke off, a perplexed frown on
her face as something Gideon had said last night came rush-
ing back to her.

'When I introduce you to the world as the star of my
next film…'

She didn't remember anything after that, so presumably
that was when she had fallen asleep. Did that mean Gideon

had carried her up to bed? Was that why she was still wearing the red dress from last night?

She gave a groan, closing her eyes.

But she was sure he had said star!

'Open the envelope, Madison,' Edgar instructed impatiently. 'Don't keep us both in suspense.'

Her hands shook with apprehension rather than suspense as she finally ripped open the envelope. Uncle Edgar was right; there was a business card inside, a card that simply had Gideon Byrne's name printed on it in gold lettering, with a telephone number underneath. Even on the business card the man's intense privacy came over quite plainly, having no address, no other adornment but that name and number.

She grimaced. 'It doesn't say anything here about calling him—'

'Look on the back, Madison,' Edgar rasped. 'There's something written there.'

The writing was large, in black ink, and read simply, 'Don't be a fool, Madison; call the number!' There was no signature, but there didn't need to be one; those eight words epitomised Gideon Byrne; he'd managed to insult her once again while at the same time issuing an order he expected to be carried out!

'Don't be a fool!' he'd written; he'd known last night that she disliked him enough to stubbornly ignore his offer of a screen-test...

But was she also stubborn enough to ignore even the remotest chance to star in a Gideon Byrne movie...?

Was she?

Madison McGuire was a fool, Gideon decided angrily as he lay in his bed staring up at the ceiling, his arms folded on the pillow behind his head. Twenty-four hours since he had left Edgar's home, and he still hadn't heard from Madison.

He had known she was stubborn, accepted that she had a temper too, remembering how those green eyes flashed on occasion. But despite what he'd put on the back of his card he hadn't really thought she was a fool…

So what did he do now?

He had been quite elated at the prospect of having found his Rosemary, had even told his assistant, Claire, all about Madison McGuire. And now, nothing. And it wasn't in his nature to go chasing after any woman, even on a professional level. So much for Edgar's machinations on Madison's behalf; maybe the older man should have spoken to Madison before setting things in motion!

But he wanted Madison to play Rosemary, damn it! And the only way he was going to achieve that, it seemed, was by seeking Madison out. Something he baulked at doing. It put him at a disadvantage from the beginning, and he wasn't in the least comfortable with that.

Damn the woman!

The telephone began to ring at his bedside. The clock read eight-thirty. Who the hell—?

But he knew. Suddenly he knew.

'Good morning,' he drawled into the receiver, his anxiety of a few minutes ago slowly receding; he didn't believe he was going to have to seek Madison out, after all…

'Mr Byrne,' Madison replied curtly. 'I realise it's early, but—I'm calling in reply to your message concerning a screen-test,' she added stiltedly.

And hating every minute of it, he realised with a half-smile. No doubt the earliness of the call was due to the fact that Madison had decided to just get the evil deed over and done with. But at least she wasn't the fool he had started to think she might be…

'Twelve o'clock today suit you?' he returned as abruptly.

There was complete silence on the other end of the telephone line, as if Madison, despite being the one to make the call, had been caught off guard.

Then she drew in a deep breath. 'That's fine,' she returned evenly. 'Edgar is driving back into the city today, so I can come in with him.'

Gideon's hand tightened about the receiver. Edgar! The man was starting to become his nemesis. 'That will be nice for you both,' he rasped. 'I'll see you at twelve o'clock—'

'You haven't told me where to go,' she put in quickly.

Because his thoughts had been on where he would like to tell *Edgar* to go! 'Edgar knows the way,' he bit out curtly. 'Don't be late,' he instructed before ringing off.

God damn it, he was no happier now that Madison had rung than he had been before when he had thought she was a little fool for not contacting him!

Edgar!

Every time he turned around that man was there. And usually at Madison's side. It did seem rather a close goddaughter/godfather relationship—

Gideon climbed out of bed impatiently. Forget Edgar. Forget Madison's relationship with the other man; he was only interested in whether or not she could really act. And he had a screen-test to organise for three hours' time. And then he would know for certain whether or not he had found his Rosemary...

Hours later, as he watched the playbacks yet again, he wasn't sure *what* he had found...!

Madison had arrived at the studio dressed in denims and a green silk shirt tucked in at her narrow waist, her hair plaited loosely down the length of her spine—and with an attitude that stood out a mile! She'd made it obvious she didn't really want to be there, as prickly as a thistle when he'd introduced her to his assistant, Claire. Although, to give Claire her due, she had done everything in her power to get Madison to relax, offering her coffee, chatting to her about how she was enjoying her stay in England so far.

None of it had helped Madison relax, and Gideon had finally had to accept that it was his own presence that was making her so edgy.

He'd excused them both to Claire, pulling Madison out of the studio. 'What the hell is wrong with you?' he snapped. 'You're here for a screen-test, not to have your teeth pulled!'

Madison gave him a look that told him she thought the latter might be preferable. 'I'm just not happy about this,' she admitted grudgingly, twisting her slender hands together in front of her.

He stood back, looking at her with narrowed eyes. Her face appeared free of make-up today, making her look even younger than she had the other evening, but the clean lines of her bone structure were clearly visible; she was absolutely stunning to look at, with or without make-up.

'Why the hell not?' he demanded harshly, annoyed with himself for not remaining as detached as he would have wished.

Madison shrugged. 'I'm not a star, Gideon—'

'Leave me to be the judge of that,' he rasped, even more determined after looking at her today that Madison could do this.

She shook her head. 'I don't want to waste your time—'

'It's my time to waste,' he insisted grimly.

For the first time today she began to look less tense, relaxing enough to give a slight smile. 'And mine,' she pointed out dryly.

He gave an inclination of his head. 'But mine is a damn sight more valuable!'

Madison smiled broadly this time. 'That's the Gideon Byrne I know,' she drawled ruefully.

He quirked dark brows. 'And love?' What the hell—? Flirting with Madison was not part of his plan. Plan! When Madison was around nothing seemed to go as he planned! 'Let's get down to business, Madison,' he continued harshly before she could make any reply. 'You do the test. You're either what I want—or we never see each other again. How does that sound?' he demanded coldly.

Her mouth twisted wryly. 'It sounds as if I should make a mess of the screen-test!'

'You may very well do that anyway,' he stated cruelly. 'Let's go and see, shall we?' He indicated they should go back into the studio.

He wasn't sure what it was—their conversation? His challenge?—but after Madison had left, and he watched the re-runs, he knew they weren't destined never to see each other again…!

She was brilliant! Her acting showed just the right amount of vulnerability, fragility—and scheming witch!— to make her the perfect Rosemary.

It was something else about Madison on the screen that bothered him. Somewhere at the back of his mind, niggling away, he knew she reminded him of someone. And he had no idea who it could be, knew he had never met anyone else, despite his dismissal at the weekend to Edgar, with Madison's particular brand of beauty. But there was something there anyway—the way she tilted her head, the curve of her cheek, a certain huskiness in her voice…

And he didn't like not knowing whoever it was she reminded him of. In fact, he felt decidedly uncomfortable as he continued to watch her on the screen.

Uncomfortable enough not to offer Madison the part…?

'Come on, Gideon.' Claire came into the studio where he still sat in the darkness. 'Let's go out and have some dinner. It's been a long day, and I'm sure you're as hungry as I am.'

It wasn't unusual for Claire and himself to end up having dinner together at the end of a long day; in fact, he spent more time with Claire than most men did with their wives! Not that he and Claire had ever thought of each other in that way; Gideon never became involved with the people he worked with—and Claire knew him too well, warts and all, to ever feel in the least bit romantic about him!

Beautiful as she was—a tall, leggy redhead in her late thirties—Claire had never married. Her career was everything to her, and as Gideon's assistant for the last five years she seemed to have found the niche she wanted. Completely to his benefit, Gideon freely acknowledged. Claire knew exactly where he should be, and when he should be there, and made sure that was exactly where he was.

She also made sure he ate properly...

'Sounds like a good idea,' he nodded, standing up, stretching stiffly. He had been sitting in the studio for hours; he needed the break.

Claire grinned. 'I booked a table at Miguel's.'

From any other woman Gideon would have seen this as an attempt to be pushy in their relationship; with Claire he was completely comfortable with the arrangement. It was a little like having a caring older sister, he decided as they left for the restaurant.

An older sister he had never had. His childhood, especially from the age of seven, had been quite a lonely one—

Damn it, he seemed to be thinking back to those days rather a lot at the moment! And considering he normally chose to keep those memories blocked out of his mind he was far from pleased at the realisation. It was Edgar, of course, with that chance remark the other day at lunch, concerning Gideon's father.

Edgar and his father had been friends, and it had been a friendship that stood the test of time—and adversity!—but it was still something Gideon would rather not have been reminded of.

In fact, he was still scowling when he and Claire reached the restaurant, completely irritated with the whole situation.

And that irritation only deepened when he saw Edgar and Madison sitting at a table together on the other side of the restaurant! Madison was looking absolutely stunning in an emerald-coloured dress that Gideon knew exactly matched those bewitching eyes he had been looking at on screen for hours!

'Great,' he muttered harshly once he and Claire had sat down, having a clear view across the room at the now laughing Madison.

Were she and Edgar already celebrating her success? And was that laughter at his expense?

Damn it, he was becoming paranoid now! He was the director of the film; he still had the power of yea or nay—

Madison's screen-test was perfect; he would be an idiot if he didn't say yea!

'Hmm?' Claire looked up at him enquiringly, already glancing through the menu.

'Nothing,' he muttered, picking up his own menu and seemingly becoming completely engrossed in it.

Which he wasn't, of course; his thoughts were all on the fact that Madison sat across the restaurant, with a man he was fast coming to dislike!

Edgar had been altogether too smug about Madison from the very first time he'd mentioned her—almost as if he were a magician producing a rabbit from a hat!

Or just a godfather producing his much loved god-daughter...?

His normal rationality had deserted him, Gideon acknowledged self-derisively. And at a time when he should be feeling elated. He had found his Rosemary, the long search was over, and he could begin work on the film now.

Then why did he still feel so uneasy about Madison's involvement in it…?

'Isn't that Madison over there?' Claire cut in on his dark thoughts. 'Oh, and Edgar Remington, too,' she recognised lightly.

Gideon barely glanced across the room at the mismatched couple; after all, he had already looked at them once; he didn't need to keep seeing them together.

'Yes,' he acknowledged tersely, his attention returning doggedly to the menu in front of him.

'She is lovely, isn't she?' Claire obviously felt no such lack of interest, her chin resting in the palm of her hand as she looked across at Madison. 'All that gorgeous blonde hair. And those emerald eyes. And she has a figure that—'

'Okay, Claire, I get the picture!' Gideon cut in harshly.

She quirked auburn brows. 'The question is; does *she*?'

His mouth twisted, his eyes narrowed irritably. 'You know damn well she does!'

Claire shrugged. 'And when do you intend telling her that?'

He scowled again. 'When I damn well feel like it!'

Claire sat back in her seat. 'Gideon, I flatter myself that I know you as well as anyone is allowed to— You're a private person—' she shrugged dismissively as he glowered fiercely 'and I respect that. As you well know, I'm pretty private myself.' She grinned knowingly; her own private life was a closed book to Gideon. 'But for some reason the mere sight of Madison McGuire seems to bring you out in invisible hives!'

He grimaced. 'Not so invisible if you can see it,' he reasoned self-derisively. 'And it isn't Madison exactly,' he sighed. 'I just—'

'Uh-oh,' Claire cut in softly. 'It appears they're just about to leave, and they're coming over.'

He had spent immeasurable hours looking at Madison on the screen, but, even so, the flesh-and-blood Madison was something else completely. As Claire had already said, Madison was gorgeous!

Male heads turned as she strolled across the restaurant at Edgar's side, her honey-coloured hair moving silkily over her shoulders and down her back, her face pale but beautiful, the green dress showing off the perfection of her figure, her legs long and shapely beneath its short skirt.

It should please him that she already attracted such attention; after all, he wanted a Rosemary that people were going to want to stare at, that people noticed in a crowd. What angered him, he inwardly acknowledged, was that most of that interest was male!

'Gideon,' Edgar greeted smoothly as he and Madison reached their table. 'And the lovely Claire,' he added huskily, bending to gallantly kiss the back of her hand. 'So nice to see you again, my dear.'

The exchange left Gideon and Madison looking wordlessly at each other, Gideon having stood up as soon as the other couple reached the table.

'Celebrating?' he rasped, at once wishing he didn't sound quite so accusing. This woman certainly brought out the worst in him!

Those green eyes flashed a warning even as her chin rose in challenge. 'Not at all,' she drawled dismissively. 'This happens to be Edgar's favourite restaurant.'

Gideon came here a lot with Claire, but he could never remember seeing the other man here before...! 'It is good.' He gave an acknowledging inclination of his head. 'Did you enjoy your meal?'

Humour glowed briefly in her deep green eyes. 'Most of it,' Madison murmured dryly.

Until he arrived, was the unspoken message Gideon read in her voice! Madison was obviously no more comfortable with him than he was with her, and he found that irritated him too. In fact, he seemed to have been in a constant state of irritation since Edgar had first mentioned Madison's name to him!

But Madison's reaction to him, this definite aversion she had to his company, wasn't one he was used to. Not that he flattered himself that women were bowled over by his irresistible charm—most people would agree that 'charm' wasn't part of his make-up!—but he wasn't unattractive, and his reputation as a film director didn't do him any harm where women were concerned, either. Madison seemed to be unimpressed with both those things…!

'How did it go today, Gideon?'

Edgar again! One of these days he was going to tell the older man exactly where to go!

As it was, Edgar had put him on the spot where today's screen-test was concerned. Not that Gideon didn't already accept that it was a *fait accompli* that Madison was to play Rosemary—he would just have preferred to tell her that in his own time, and in his own way!

It was the look of dismay on Madison's face as she looked incredulously at Edgar that made Gideon relent slightly. 'I think that's for Madison and I to discuss, don't you?' he challenged the older man; the sooner Edgar got his interfering nose out of this, the better he would like it!

The older man shrugged unconcernedly. 'Obviously Madison hasn't had time to find herself an agent over here yet, and so—'

'With you around she doesn't need one!' Gideon found himself interrupting, turning impatiently to Madison. 'Come in and see me tomorrow,' he bit out abruptly. 'About the same time as today?' He looked questioningly at Claire, who gave an affirmative nod of her head. 'We can discuss a contract.'

Madison's gaze was steady as she looked at him. 'Does that mean I got the part?'

Still Gideon felt reluctant to commit himself to that! What on earth was wrong with him? He had been looking for exactly the right person for this film for months now, and now that he had finally found her he didn't seem able to admit as much. He wasn't offering to marry the girl, for goodness' sake, just to have her star in his next film!

'Gideon wouldn't be wasting his time on you if you hadn't,' Edgar put in dryly. 'Would you, Gideon?' he added challengingly.

Edgar was so damned determined...!

Gideon's uneasiness of earlier, as he'd watched Madison on that screen, returned with a vengeance. What the hell was he getting himself involved in? Whatever it was, it was too late now; the moment he'd seen Madison he had become involved!

His mouth twisted wryly. 'It means we're going to discuss the possibility of a contract,' he insisted stubbornly. He might only be delaying the inevitable, but it was his film, his contract, his star; he would do this in his way, or not at all.

Madison continued to look at him for several long seconds, and then she turned away, smiling constrainedly at Edgar. 'I think it's time we left and let Gideon and Claire get on with their dinner, don't you?' She linked her arm with his. 'Nice to see you again, Claire,' she added warmly.

The two men exchanged nods, Edgar's smoothly confident, Gideon's coldly dismissive, his eyes narrowed as he watched Edgar and Madison walk away.

'You're letting your antagonism show,' Claire drawled softly.

Gideon turned to her sharply, the two of them resuming their seats. He shook his head. 'Edgar is—'

'I didn't mean Edgar,' Claire cut in, brows raised in query.

He frowned, that frown deepening as Claire's meaning became clear. 'I don't know Madison McGuire well enough to feel antagonistic towards her,' he rasped dismissively.

'I thought that,' Claire replied lightly, continuing to meet his gaze.

'Don't get clever on me, Claire,' he scorned derisively; their five-year working relationship gave Claire a lot of leeway where he was concerned, but making ambiguous comments concerning his behaviour was overstepping the line.

Damn it, it wasn't Claire he was angry with! It was—it was— Hell, he didn't even know who he was angry with any more!

'Let's order our food,' he suggested harshly, putting a firm end to that conversation.

But that didn't mean he had forgotten about it as they ordered and ate their meal...

Or when he returned alone to his apartment later that evening.

What was it about Madison McGuire that made him so angry? Hell, he didn't know! But one thing he did know: he would have to get that anger under firm control before they began working together...

CHAPTER FOUR

'I'M REALLY sorry about this, Madison.' Claire grimaced as she came back into the room.

For what had to be the fourth time!

Madison had arrived at the studio at exactly twelve o'clock, as requested, been shown to a sitting-room by the ever friendly Claire—and she had remained sitting here for forty minutes waiting for Gideon Byrne to put in an appearance!

If he was hoping to unnerve her by keeping her waiting in this way, he was going to be sadly disappointed; she was furious at his tardiness. He might be the great Gideon Byrne, but good manners cost him nothing, and if he wasn't able to meet the twelve o'clock appointment after all he should have damn well telephoned and told her so!

'He's definitely in the studio somewhere,' Claire continued awkwardly. 'We arrived together over two hours ago. Could I get you another cup of coffee?' she offered hopefully.

'No, thanks.' Madison stood up, slinging her bag over her shoulder in preparation for leaving. 'Gideon is obviously busy, and I—'

'Oh, please don't leave.' Claire touched her arm. 'I'm sure Gideon will be here in just a few minutes.'

Then she had more confidence in him than Madison did! He was a boor, a rude, arrogant boor, and as such he could take his film role and shove—

'Sorry I'm a little late, ladies!' The object of her anger strolled unhurriedly into the room, the air immediately filled with that charge of electricity he took around with him, his dark brows raised as he took in the fact that Madison was standing, her stance aggressive, obviously preparing to leave. 'Your contract.' He held up some of the papers he had in his hand. 'It took a little longer to—prepare than I had anticipated.'

Her contract... She had begun to wonder, with his lack of appearance, whether Gideon Byrne wasn't playing some elaborately cruel hoax on her by asking her to come here today.

She hadn't wanted to come here at all; she was sure she and Gideon could never work together. But, as Uncle Edgar had pointed out, opportunities like this one didn't happen every day. In fact, if she refused this one, it might never happen again! And so she had gritted her teeth, chosen carefully the conservative emerald-coloured suit she was wearing matched with a cream blouse, brushed her hair until it shone like molten gold, and arrived here promptly at twelve o'clock.

Only to be kept waiting by Gideon Byrne for forty minutes!

'Did you book the table for lunch?' he asked Claire, obviously having felt no pressure to dress smartly himself for their appointment. He was wearing a pair of black denims similar to the ones he had been wearing the first time she'd met him, this time with a black silk shirt. There was no doubting his rugged attractiveness, but he was hardly dressed for the formal business meeting Madison had been expecting.

And now he seemed more concerned about his lunch than he did about their meeting! Perhaps this was all a joke after all!

Madison straightened, the two-inch heels of her black shoes adding height to her five feet eight inches, her chin tilted, giving her a regal appearance as she looked at

Gideon through narrowed lids. 'Please don't let me keep you,' she drawled coldly. 'I'm sure—'

'Of course you're invited for lunch, Madison,' Gideon cut in dismissively, before turning to Claire once again. 'Did you order the taxi?'

By 'invited to lunch' Madison supposed he had to mean she was going to join them for lunch!

It would have been nice to have been asked if she was free to join them, but the more she came to know of Gideon, the more she realised this man didn't ask anything; he ordered or he took! Maybe his mother had overcompensated for the break-up between his father and herself, and given the young Gideon whatever he wanted so that he didn't feel his father's loss; whatever the reason, he was an incredibly arrogant man!

And as for his treatment of Claire...! The other woman might be his personal assistant, and so paid to work for him—she would need to be very highly paid, Madison would have thought!—but surely he could say please and thank you occasionally...?

'Waiting outside,' Claire confirmed dryly, obviously used to Gideon's manner, although she shot Madison a rueful smile as she seemed to guess what she was thinking.

'Let's go,' Gideon muttered grimly, placing a hand under Madison's elbow as he guided her out of the sitting-room and down the corridor towards the entrance.

Madison glanced back to give Claire a rueful smile of her own, only to find the other woman wasn't following them, that she was actually nowhere in sight. Did that mean she was having lunch with Gideon alone?

'What is it?' He glanced down at her, having obviously felt her increased tension at that realisation, but not altering the speed of his own lengthy stride towards the double glass doors that led outside, still taking Madison along with him.

How did she even try to explain to this man that she had

come to England for a relaxing holiday with her uncle Edgar after a rather traumatic time both emotionally and professionally, and that since her arrival, and meeting Gideon Byrne, she had felt as if she was on an express train? And she wasn't sure of its destination! What she did know, and found extremely unnerving, was that Gideon himself seemed to be at the controls!

'Nothing,' she said wearily. What was the point of explaining anything to this man? His interest in her was purely professional. She would be even more agitated if it were anything else!

There was no doubting that Gideon was a physically attractive man, or that a lot of women would find his arrogance added to that attraction, but as far as Madison was concerned she preferred someone a little more gentle, with more consideration, someone who—

Someone like Gerry? She mocked her own gullibility over that particular relationship. She'd been completely taken in by his supposed gentleness and consideration—right up until the time he dumped her for a clinging red-head, who was coincidentally the sister of the director of his next play. At least with someone like Gideon, what you saw was what you got!

And she, for one, didn't want it!

Neither did she want to be bundled into the taxi, completely ignored on the short drive to the Chinese restaurant—and, as he hadn't consulted her on his choice of restaurant, he obviously didn't give a damn whether or not she actually liked Chinese food! Then she found herself seated next to Gideon in a secluded booth at the back of the room, a screen covered in Chinese art placed in front of their table and so blocking out the rest of the busy restaurant, leaving Madison with only Gideon to look at. Wonderful!

'The Chinese understand more than most the need for

privacy,' Gideon drawled as he easily read her thoughts. 'Read this.' He dropped the contract on to the table in front of her. 'I'll order the food.' He picked up the menu.

There appeared to be pages and pages of 'this', and Madison had no intention of going through all of the contract—especially the small print!—while she ate her lunch. She wasn't that naive; she intended letting her godfather look through it before she signed anything.

Besides, she was quite capable of ordering her own food!

She picked up the contract and carefully placed it on the table in front of Gideon. 'You tell me what it says,' she told him with saccharine sweetness. 'And *I'll* order our food!' She met his gaze challengingly and he frowned at her.

Gideon continued to look at her wordlessly for several long seconds, and then he slowly began to smile, that smile that transformed him from austerely attractive to devilishly handsome, before shrugging his shoulders. 'Nothing with ginger in it for me,' he murmured dryly, that dark grey gaze appreciative as he seemed to take in her appearance for the first time today.

Madison looked quickly down at the menu, but she could feel the heat in her cheeks from that suddenly appreciative gaze. Damn him; most of the time he gave the impression he was nothing but a machine, with about as much emotion, and then suddenly he became sensually male, making her very aware of him as a man, but also making her very aware of her own femininity.

She could feel the sudden hardening of her nipples now, against the silk of her blouse, in response to his maleness. Her only consolation was that because she still wore her jacket he couldn't possibly be aware of that response.

Although she didn't feel so confident of that when she glanced up seconds later and found his gaze on that betraying part of her anatomy, a lazy smile curving those sensual lips now!

She closed the menu with a decisive snap. This man was still playing with her, and—

'Decided already?' he drawled huskily.

She opened her mouth to tell him exactly what she had decided, only to find the waiter hovering beside their table waiting to take their order. Okay, he had said no ginger, but he had said nothing about the hot dishes on the menu, and she deliberately ordered half a dozen of them. Let's see if he's still smiling after that lot, she decided angrily.

'Exactly what I would have ordered myself.' He nodded in approval of her choices. 'With lots of mineral water,' he told the waiter lightly before he left to process their order.

Of course, he didn't drink alcohol. Madison wasn't a great lover of it herself, but right now she could have done with a stiff whisky—or two!

'Now to get down to the contract.' Gideon was suddenly all cold efficiency once again. 'I'll read through it, and then you can tell me if you have any comments, okay?'

She nodded her agreement. But she still intended letting Edgar look at it before she signed anything. Besides, she hadn't even seen the whole film script yet, as Gideon had only given her two precious pages of it for her screen-test the day before. As if he didn't trust anyone with all of it…!

Although she had a feeling the thick envelope he'd carried with him from the studio and placed carefully on the bench-seat beside him when he'd sat down a few minutes ago might just be that script, so maybe he was going to part with it, after all… And she was sure Edgar, as her protective godfather, wouldn't have let her go this far if he didn't approve of the script himself…?

Half an hour later Gideon was still reading through the contract. Their food had been delivered, and was being duly eaten—with not a sign of discomfort at the hot spices on Gideon's part, Madison noticed with regret.

Because there was certainly a lot of discomfort on her part as regards the contract; she didn't need Edgar to look at it to know there were several paragraphs in it she didn't like in the least!

'Will I be allowed to breathe without your say-so?' she taunted when Gideon finally got to the end of it.

'As long as it's only shallowly,' he returned dryly.

'That's what I thought.' She nodded. 'Gideon, you can't seriously expect me to sign something like that—'

'I'm very serious, Madison,' he cut in harshly. 'I have deliberately chosen an unknown for this film—you! And I don't wish that unknown—'

'Me,' she put in derisively.

'You,' he agreed coldly. 'I don't want you giving unauthorised interviews—in fact talking to the press for any reason, and certainly providing no opportunity for them to take photographs. The fact that you are unknown adds to the mystery of the film.' His eyes were metallic in his seriousness.

She shook her head. 'I understand that bit—I think. But—and correct me if I'm wrong—it also says in there that I'm not to talk to anyone about the film. Anyone at all. Gideon, I have a family—'

'A mother, father and brother,' he remembered correctly.

'Exactly,' Madison confirmed impatiently, not in the least impressed with his power of recall. 'Do you seriously expect that I can get away with not telling them what I'm doing for the next—eight months, isn't it?' She referred back to the contract.

'Longer if we overrun our schedule.' He nodded grimly.

'Whatever.' She gave a dismissive wave of her hand. 'My brother would be over here with a shotgun if I disappeared off the face of the earth for that length of time!'

Gideon's mouth twisted mockingly. 'I wouldn't call going to the Isle of Man disappearing off the face of the earth!' He named the intended location for shooting the majority of the film.

Her eyes flashed deeply green at that mockery. 'I doubt my brother has ever heard of it!' She hadn't herself until Gideon had explained it was a picturesque island situated in the Irish Sea, halfway between England and Ireland!

'He's your older brother?' Gideon asked derisively.

'My only brother,' she corrected him impatiently. 'And he—'

'And your father is Malcolm McGuire,' he continued thoughtfully. 'Compliments of Edgar,' he shrugged at her sharp look. 'What's your mother called?'

'Mrs McGuire!' she snapped angrily; he was being deliberately irritating!

Gideon gave one of those chuckles that made him look almost warmly human. Almost. Because Madison knew that within seconds that could easily change…!

'Just natural curiosity, Madison.' He shrugged dismissively. 'You're close to your family?'

She thought of her tall, strong father, her petite, beautiful mother, her handsome older brother. 'Very,' she murmured softly. She missed them all already, indeed, it felt as if it was weeks rather than days since she had last seen them all!

'Hmm.' Gideon nodded. 'Then you're right; that could obviously pose a problem…'

A problem! It was ridiculous to ask anyone to— 'Does anyone else with a part in the film have a clause like that one in their contract?' She looked at him with narrowed eyes. 'Do you?'

'It doesn't apply to me,' he bit out harshly. 'For one thing, I'm the director. And for another—I don't have any family to be close to!'

None at all? She knew his father had died years ago, but was his mother dead too...? How sad; Gideon was only in his late thirties, and yet he was already alone in the world...

Good heavens; sympathy was the last thing this man wanted, from her or anyone else!

She shook her head. 'I'm sorry about that. But I believe that clause to be unreasonable—'

'So unreasonable you aren't willing to sign the contract?' Gideon looked at her through narrowed eyes.

Was this a trap? Did Gideon not want her to sign the contract, and so not be in the film, either...?

He was certainly objectionable enough, was constantly rude to her, seemed to be grudgingly offering her the part of Rosemary—

Edgar...!

She was American, Rosemary was English. She had been in only one other film, and that a very minor part, and, even though Gideon claimed he wanted an unknown, wasn't she just a little too much of an unknown? Added to all that, her godfather was the owner of the company that was producing the film...

She straightened in her chair, picking up her handbag. 'I believe we are wasting each other's time, Gideon,' she told him stiltedly. 'And we both know how valuable your time is!' she added bitterly, standing up to leave.

Gideon stood up too. 'Madison—'

'Please, Gideon!' She was very much afraid she was about to cry! And that was the last thing she wanted to do in front of this man. There had been too many disappointments in her life of late, and this latest cruelty felt like the last straw.

But before she could turn to leave she felt her arms taken in a firm grasp, with Gideon shaking her slightly. 'I have no idea what direction your thoughts are running in—although I could probably make an educated guess!' he said harshly. 'Let me assure you, no one tells me what to do!'

Her tears were blinding her now. 'Edgar—'

'Least of all Edgar,' he dismissed scornfully, no longer shaking her, his hands almost gentle on her arms now. 'Madison…!'

Maybe if she hadn't been blinded by the tears she would have seen the kiss coming, but as it was she was completely unprepared for the force of Gideon's mouth coming down on hers.

Unprepared…! There was no way she could have foreseen Gideon kissing her. And in a public restaurant of all places, albeit behind the privacy of a screen.

Nor foreseen her own response to that kiss…!

It was as if she had been waiting for this moment since they'd first met at the pool, electricity fusing them together, mouths moving erotically together, bodies pressed together, in perfect unison. Madison's senses reeled as she clung to the warm strength of Gideon's shoulders.

'What the hell am I doing…?' Gideon had wrenched his mouth from hers, his fingers biting into her arms now as he held her away from him, his expression grimly contemptuous. 'Take the damned contract, Madison.' He thrust it at her. 'Talk it over with Edgar.' His mouth twisted. 'I'm sure you'll find that he can see nothing wrong with it!'

It was his contempt that stung her the most. After all, he had been the one to instigate the kiss, not her. 'He isn't the one signing it!' she snapped.

Gideon bent to pick up the thick padded envelope. 'Take this, too,' he rasped. 'Maybe it will help you make up your mind! I hardly need say it's for your eyes only,' he added with hard derision.

The closely guarded film script… 'Thank you for lunch—I think,' she muttered before walking away, the contract and script clutched in her shaking hands.

Her legs were shaking too, but they did support her all the way outside the restaurant and into a taxi. She leaned back against the seat as she expelled a shaky breath.

Having Gideon Byrne kiss her had been the last thing on her mind today. Her only conclusion was that she was sure it had been the last thing on Gideon's mind too...

Damn it, he had just kissed Madison McGuire!

And he had enjoyed it too. Madison might be slender, but she was softly curvaceous to hold, and her mouth...! Despite the spicy food they had both eaten, Madison had tasted of peaches and cream, her lips softly responsive, so much so that desire had made him forget briefly exactly where they were.

He shook his head in self-disgust, dropping back down into his chair. A public restaurant, for goodness' sake.

Hell, it didn't matter where it had happened; he had kissed an actress he intended working very closely with. And already he knew that brief intimacy was going to cause trouble between the two of them. If Madison should decide to sign the contract...

If.

That was the question that needed answering now. He shouldn't have let his reluctance to work with Madison show when he was talking to her, but it was very difficult to control his wariness whenever he was around her for any length of time. And, for reasons he didn't completely understand himself, he *was* reluctant; even the knowledge that she would make a perfect Rosemary couldn't dispel that uneasy feeling. And Madison had sensed that...

He was still scowling when he returned to the office a couple of hours later. Claire was busy working, although she looked up when he walked into the room.

She pulled a face at his frown. 'Oh, dear, Gideon; what have you done to the beautiful Madison now?' she taunted.

He stiffened resentfully. 'What makes you think I've done anything to her?'

Claire grinned. 'Could it be the fact that Edgar Remington telephoned here not long ago threatening murder?'

Gideon grimaced. 'Mine, of course!'

'Of course.' Her grin widened. 'I told him he would have to get in line!' She shrugged.

'Thanks!' Gideon sat on the edge of the desk, picking up a paperweight from the desk-top, playing with it distractedly. 'What else did he have to say?'

Claire sighed, thinking. 'Well, quite a lot of it was unrepeatable, but the main gist of the conversation was that if you want Madison in your film you had better apologise to her first—and take out Clause 27 from the contract!'

Gideon drew in an angry breath. Apologise! For what? For kissing her? The woman was twenty-two years old—surely she hadn't gone running to her godfather with tales of having been kissed? Certainly not against her will; he might have his own reasons for regretting that kiss, but he certainly hadn't imagined Madison's response to it...!

'Clause 27...?' Claire prompted interestedly.

Clause 27. The clause that said Madison couldn't discuss the film with anyone. It was the reason he'd been late for their appointment earlier; he had been busy getting Clause 27 through his lawyers. And it was legal. It was just, as Madison had pointed out only too clearly, 'unreasonable'.

He gave a heavy sigh. 'Never mind,' he dismissed harshly. 'I presume Edgar also had some suggestion as to how I should make this apology to his god-daughter?' he prompted disgustedly.

'I got the clear impression that on your knees would do,' Claire teased.

'In his dreams!' Gideon rasped, standing up abruptly. 'I

don't need Madison McGuire that badly!' He turned to leave.

'Don't you…?' Claire called out softly.

He turned back sharply. 'No!' he bit out harshly; he didn't need *anyone* that badly! 'Now would you just—?' He broke off as the telephone began to ring on the desk. 'If it's Edgar for me—I'm out!' He strode purposefully out of the room, heading for the kitchen.

Right now he wished he did drink alcohol, but as he didn't he would have to make do with strong coffee! He had barely poured the coffee from the pot into a mug when Claire appeared in the kitchen doorway. The grim expression on his face should have been enough to deter her, but she merely grinned at him unconcernedly. A typical example of familiarity breeding a lack of respect, Gideon acknowledged moodily.

'There's a Madison McGuire on the telephone— Control it, Gideon,' Claire warned as he slammed his mug down savagely on the worktop before striding from the kitchen to take the call. 'Try listening to what she has to say before you explode,' Claire called after him, remaining in the kitchen and leaving him to take the call in privacy.

He grabbed up the receiver. 'Yes?' he demanded resentfully.

If Madison thought she could set her godfather on him, and then just phone up here and expect to hear him grovelling, then she was in for a surprise. He didn't grovel to anyone, let alone some—

'Gideon, I believe I owe you an apology.' Madison spoke in that gentle American drawl.

It deflated him like a punctured balloon! *She* owed *him* an apology…?

This whole situation, he inwardly acknowledged, was ricocheting out of control. And it wasn't a feeling Gideon was in the least bit comfortable with!

'I thought that was supposed to be my line!' he came back scornfully.

Madison sighed softly. 'Uncle Edgar—overreacted earlier, when I was—less than controlled, when I returned from our meeting.' She was obviously choosing her words carefully. 'But I had no idea, until a short time ago, that he'd actually telephoned you. I—I've signed the contract and will have it brought over to you by special courier,' she added hesitantly. 'It should arrive some time later this afternoon.'

Gideon was stunned. There was no other word for it. Madison McGuire, unlike most women, was a complete puzzle to him. She had been upset about the contract earlier, and Edgar had obviously agreed with her objections— and now she called and told him she'd signed the damned thing, without a single change having been made! Unpredictable, irrational—

'I can read your thoughts, Gideon,' Madison murmured in a wryly amused voice, so that he was able to visualise that soft curve of her lips as she smiled.

'I doubt it,' he drawled ruefully. 'Have you read the film script?' he prompted shrewdly; no actress who thought anything of her career at all would be able to turn down a part like Rosemary if it were offered to her. Maybe that was the reason Madison had signed the contract…?

'Not yet.' Madison completely disabused him of that theory. 'I— Uncle Edgar had no right to interfere; I'm quite capable of fighting my own battles,' she added hardly.

Gideon smiled to himself now, able to imagine Edgar's incredulity when Madison told him that! And now he *did* know the reason why Madison had signed the contract: stubborn pride. Well, he had enough of that himself, so maybe he did understand her, after all…

But not too much! After all, he had behaved completely out of character earlier when he'd kissed her. And now she had signed the contract the two of them were going to be constantly together for the next eight months at least…

'Famous last words, Madison,' he drawled mockingly.

There was only the briefest of pauses. 'I don't think so,' she came back confidently.

Only time would tell. And time together appeared to be something they were going to have plenty of.

CHAPTER FIVE

MADISON slowly put down her telephone receiver, knowing she hadn't been completely honest with Gideon just now. It was true she hadn't read the film script, not all of it, but she had glanced through it—enough to know it was brilliant, the most emotionally exciting female role to come along in a very long time.

But what she found most amazing about it was that its author was Gideon Byrne...!

She'd been so angry with herself when she got back, for responding to Gideon's kiss, that she hadn't looked at the script for some time. But once she had...!

She'd decided she was going to forget that kiss, to act as if it had never happened. It was the only way she and Gideon would ever be able to work together.

And they would be working together; there was no way she could turn down the opportunity to play a character as complex as Rosemary. In fact, she was past caring what influence Edgar may or may not have brought to bear to secure the part for her; she wanted to play Rosemary!

How had Gideon ever written such a screenplay? Madison didn't doubt that Gideon knew women well—some of them probably too well!—but Rosemary was actually two women, Rose and Mary, with two distinct sides to the character, one good, one evil, but both with that grey shade that could make those two things hard to distinguish.

It was those shades of grey that made the climax to the film so breathtaking.

She looked up sharply as a knock sounded softly on her bedroom door; she didn't need two guesses as to who it would be! 'Come in, Uncle Edgar,' she invited. 'Were you listening in on the extension downstairs?' she mocked derisively as her godfather entered the room.

'Of course not,' he dismissed impatiently, moving to sit uninvited on the end of her bed. 'But I do hope you haven't done anything stupid?' He looked at her pointedly.

She quirked blonde brows. 'Such as turn down the part?'

'Madison—'

'I believe I told you at the weekend that I'm not stupid, Uncle Edgar,' she cut in. 'Stubborn, hot-headed, sometimes over-sentimental—'

'Just like your mother,' he acknowledged affectionately.

'But never stupid.' Madison shook her head decisively.

'I wish I could say the same for your mother—if she'd had any sense it would have been me she married thirty years ago!' he explained at Madison's questioning look.

She gave a rueful smile; Edgar had never made any secret of the fact that he believed her mother should have been his wife. 'It happened to be my father she fell in love with.'

'Hmm.' He stood up impatiently, frowning. 'I'm expecting a call from her within the next hour; she will, of course, want to speak to you.'

'And I can't tell her anything!' Madison groaned.

'I told you not to sign that damned contract.' Edgar scowled darkly. 'Gideon has no right to ask you for such an agreement—'

'I thought we agreed earlier that we wouldn't talk about the movie any more, either, Uncle Edgar?' she interrupted, her brows raised pointedly.

The argument that had followed her realisation that he had interfered, by telephoning Gideon, had not been a pleasant one. The only thing that had stopped her immediately moving out to a hotel had been Edgar's promise that he wouldn't interfere again. She certainly didn't want to have to go through apologising to Gideon ever again!

'We did,' he acknowledged grudgingly. 'But how are we going to explain things to your mother? As I understand it, Gideon will want you to be in the Isle of Man within the next month or so; what am I supposed to tell your mother when she telephones here and wants to talk to you?' He didn't look exactly overjoyed at the prospect.

Madison could easily understand why. Her mother was very protective of both her children, and had asked Edgar to take care of her only daughter while she was in England. She would not appreciate being told Madison had gone off somewhere!

'We'll think of something when the time comes, Uncle Edgar,' she assured him dismissively. 'In the meantime, there's nothing to tell.' She shrugged.

He shook his head. 'Maybe I should just never have got you involved.' He sighed worriedly. 'But at the time it seemed like too good an opportunity to miss,' he muttered distractedly.

Madison moved to give him a brief hug. 'Starring in a Gideon Byrne movie *is* too good an opportunity to miss!' she told him lightly. She was even willing to put aside her own aversion to the man, now that she had seen the script!

His mouth twisted wryly. 'Your mother may not agree with us!'

She linked her arm through his. 'I told you, we'll deal with Mom together when the times comes.'

Edgar didn't look any more confident about doing that than Madison actually felt. Her mother was the easiest-going person imaginable, unless provoked, in which case the person doing the provoking had better watch out!

But Madison didn't have too much time to think of her mother during the next few weeks, or of what her reaction would be when she discovered what her daughter was up to, as Madison was caught up in a whirl of costume fittings, make-up and hair appointments, all arranged for her by the ever attendant Claire. Gideon had apparently already gone to the Isle of Man to film outside shots that didn't need Madison in them.

And when she wasn't busy at one appointment or another Madison worked with Claire on trying to memorise the script. No easy task, considering the size of the part, and as the days passed, and the time for her to go to the island came closer, she began to wonder if she was really up to this. It was one thing being offered and accepting the part, quite another actually playing it. And Gideon would never forgive her if she let him down!

And, if she were honest, it was his displeasure she feared the most. He had written the screenplay, intended to direct it too, obviously believed in it very deeply. If she were the reason it wasn't the success he hoped for, Gideon would never forgive her.

While she was in this state of nerves, it was not the best of times for Madison to be told by Claire that Gideon was coming back to London for a couple of days and that he expected Madison to fly back to the island with him!

Claire easily read the dismay on her face; in fact, the two women had become quite good friends over the last three weeks—which was just as well when they had to spend so much time together.

'Gideon's bark is much worse than his bite,' Claire assured her. The two women were in the office, having just returned from yet another fitting for the numerous clothes Madison's role seemed to require.

She grimaced. 'It's his bark most people hear.'

Claire laughed softly. 'It's more often a roar—but I wouldn't worry about it,' she added hastily as Madison looked less than happy. 'The trick with Gideon is—' She broke off, looking pointedly towards the open doorway. 'Good afternoon, Gideon,' she greeted dryly.

The subject of their conversation leant nonchalantly against the doorframe, a sardonic smile curving those chiselled lips. '''The trick with Gideon''…?' he prompted softly.

'Never let him know what you're thinking,' Claire came back instantly, not thrown for even an instant by his unexpected arrival.

Unlike Madison, who'd jumped up out of the chair as soon as she'd seen him, looking apprehensively at him now as he sauntered into the room. Gideon's hair had grown over the last three weeks, and was dark and wavy over his shirt collar, and there was a ruggedness to his features, but the grey of his eyes had their usual arctic chill as his gaze swept over her critically.

'And what *are* you thinking, Madison McGuire?' he drawled speculatively. 'Did you let someone cut your hair?' he demanded before she could formulate an answer to his first question, his gaze narrowed on her now.

She put her hand up self-consciously. 'Only the fringe. Claire—' She swallowed hard, deciding against involving the other woman; after all, she had told Gideon she could fight her own battles! 'I—'

'It makes you look younger,' he bit out tersely. 'Excellent.' He nodded his satisfaction.

'Are you through terrifying the life out of her?' Claire put in with irony. 'Or shall I just wait until you have?'

Gideon turned mockingly to Madison. 'I'm not terrifying you, am I?'

She stiffened defensively. He was everything she remembered—and more. She hadn't actually seen him since that day in the restaurant, when he'd kissed her, and the memory of that kiss gave an extra flush to her cheeks. 'Not in the least,' she replied dismissively, meeting his gaze with a challenge of her own.

'See?' He turned to Claire, strolling further into the room. 'I'm glad you're here, actually, Madison; it will save me the bother of a telephone call.'

'And goodness knows we need to cut financial corners wherever we can,' Claire put in with soft sarcasm.

Gideon shot her a scathing glance. 'If you weren't so damned indispensable…!'

Claire grinned unconcernedly. 'To what do we owe the honour of your company two days ahead of schedule?'

Madison had wondered, when she'd first met Claire, whether the other woman might not secretly be in love with her employer—after all, not everyone found him as irritating as she did herself, and Claire seemed to take his rudeness completely in her stride. But a couple of days into her closer acquaintance with Claire and she realised the older woman viewed him more as a naughty older brother than anything else. Madison didn't quite see him in that light, herself, but Claire certainly knew him better than she did…!

Not that Claire's attitude to Gideon precluded his being attracted to her, Madison realised for the first time. Gideon was obviously completely comfortable in Claire's company, and there was no doubting that the other woman was extremely beautiful…

Gideon grinned. 'I'm back early so that I can take Madison to the cinema this evening!'

What on earth was he talking about? Even supposing she wished to go, it was—

'The film première of *Eagle's Rest*,' Claire told Madison knowingly.

She blinked her surprise, at the same time realising how naive she had been to think Gideon was actually inviting her out on a date; everything this man did involved his

work in some way! He needed a female partner for this
film première, and he already knew her well enough to
realise she wouldn't see anything romantic in his invitation.
Everything this man did had an ulterior motive!

Except that kiss…

She pushed that kiss to the back of her mind—where it
belonged! 'I thought I was supposed to keep a low profile…?' And accompanying Gideon to a film première was
guaranteed to do the opposite of that! Besides, she wasn't
sure she wanted to spend the evening with him; in fact, she
knew she didn't!

'You are.' Gideon nodded with satisfaction. 'But Claire
tells me you've been working hard; I thought you could do
with a night out.'

'I thought you'd more or less decided against going to
the première?' Claire was obviously as puzzled as Madison.

'It isn't only a woman's prerogative to change her mind,'
Gideon answered dismissively. 'You didn't cancel my invitation, did you?'

'Now, would I do that without direct instruction from
you?' Claire came back.

'No,' he conceded. 'Anyway, I decided Madison might
enjoy the experience,' he added lightly.

'You're all heart, Gideon!' Madison derided.

Madison was sure his change of mind had nothing to do
with his heart—in fact, she seriously doubted he had ever
been issued with that part of the anatomy! And attending
this film première, as Gideon's partner, didn't sound like
something she would 'enjoy' at all.

From what she could gather, Gideon was rarely photo-
graphed with a woman at his side, and arriving at such an
occasion with a mystery woman on his arm was sure to
intrigue the public.

'Your attendance will provide free publicity and specu-
lation about *Rosemary*!' Madison realised ruefully.

'What...?' Gideon turned to her frowning, his brows clearing as he nodded. 'You see, you're already thinking like a star!'

She was doing no such thing; she was merely coming to realise how this man's mind worked—deviously! No doubt, apart from the people involved in this evening's film, most of the interest would focus on Gideon himself, because of his usual non-appearance at such public events. Although there was sure to be curiosity about his partner for the evening too. A curiosity Madison would no doubt enjoy blocking.

'Wear that red dress you wore at Edgar's a few weeks ago,' Gideon continued arrogantly. 'It suits you. And leave your hair loose,' he told her with critical appraisal. 'And not too much make-up; I don't like painted dolls,' he added grimly.

Madison looked at him with blazing green eyes. Who the hell did he think he was?

'It's usual to leave a woman's choice of dress to her, Gideon,' Claire put in hastily as she saw the angry colour mounting in Madison's cheeks. 'And I'm sure Madison is more than capable of dressing suitably for the occasion,' she added, with a placating smile in Madison's direction.

Madison was grateful for the other woman's words of encouragement, but at this moment she could cheerfully have knocked that arrogant smile off Gideon's sculptured lips! How dared he tell her what to wear, and how to do her hair and make-up? When he directed her in the film he might have the right to do that, but tonight was her own time, and she would damn well dress and look how she liked!

She gave Gideon a saccharine smile as she picked up her bag in preparation for leaving. 'In that case, I had better go home and get myself ready.'

Gideon nodded slowly, looking at her with narrowed eyes. 'Are you staying at Edgar's house in town?'

Her head went back as she met his gaze defiantly. 'Of course.' Did he still have a problem with that…?

He nodded grimly. 'I'll call for you there at seven o'clock.'

Yes, he obviously did still have a problem with her relationship with Edgar. Oh, well, that was his problem, not hers.

She had a film première to 'suitably' dress for!

'I would be careful how far you push her, Gideon,' Claire murmured softly, gazing after Madison. 'One thing I've learnt about Madison these last three weeks is that she has a definite mind of her own!'

Gideon had watched Madison leave too; she was even more beautiful than he remembered!

Madison had accepted the excuse that he had come back earlier than expected because he wanted to attend the film première this evening, after all. The truth was much deeper than that.

He'd been in the Isle of Man for three weeks, and not a day had gone by when he hadn't thought of Madison and the kiss they'd shared…!

He was thirty-eight years old, of course there had been women in his life, but none that had lingered in his mind when he wasn't with her. He'd only *kissed* Madison McGuire, and yet he couldn't get her out of his mind!

And so he'd come back, using the excuse of the film première this evening, even to himself, only to be totally thrown when he'd found Madison here at his office with Claire. Maybe he had been a bit tough on Madison, as Claire said, but he hadn't expected to see her quite that soon after his arrival.

'She can take it,' he dismissed.

Claire turned to look at him scathingly. 'You look like hell,' she told him bluntly.

'Thanks!' He ran a hand through his overlong hair, smiling ruefully at his assistant as he turned to leave. 'If my ego ever gets too inflated I'll just come and talk to you!'

'If!' Claire called after him pointedly.

He laughed softly as he went to his office, but that laughter faded as soon as he shut the door behind him.

Madison McGuire; what the hell was he going to do with her...?

He knew what he wanted to do with her three hours later when he called for her at Edgar's apartment—but, with Edgar standing protectively in the background, carrying her off to bed and making love to her was obviously out of the question!

Madison looked absolutely stunning!

Her dress—not the red one he had asked her to wear—was a mixture of shimmering silver and the palest of green, the material clinging to her body as she moved, darkening her eyes to emerald, her hair to a rich silver-gold; the latter was worn loose as he had requested, but in a long abundance of curls that cascaded down the length of her spine.

She might not be dressed as he had requested, but she was the most beautiful woman he had ever seen in his life!

'I thought you assured me there was no such thing as mermaids,' he murmured appreciatively.

Madison moistened coral-painted lips. 'I—'

'My God, Gideon, if I didn't know you better, I would have said that almost sounded romantic!'

Gideon turned glittering grey eyes on the older man; he wished Edgar a million miles away. He could do without his mockery at this particular moment!

Or could he? If he'd sounded romantic to Edgar just now, goodness knew what he would have said next! And Madison was not a woman he should become involved with.

For the next eight months, anyway…!

His mouth twisted scornfully. 'Don't be ridiculous, Edgar,' he snapped derisively. 'Are you ready?' He turned back to Madison. 'I think we should try and arrive before the royal guest of honour, don't you?'

She looked at him. 'And here was me thinking that was you!' she drawled mockingly, her gaze admiring his own appearance in the black dinner suit and snowy white shirt.

Gideon looked back at her with narrowed eyes, and Edgar's explosion of laughter—at his expense!—was not conducive to him holding on to his temper, either! Well, he couldn't say Claire hadn't warned him; obviously telling Madison earlier how to dress for the evening hadn't gone down too well…!

'That's next year,' he drawled.

Madison's smile faded as Edgar helped her on with her short silver-coloured jacket, causing Gideon to look at her with questioning eyes. What had he said to make her lose her sense of humour…?

'Have fun, children,' Edgar encouraged as they turned to leave.

'Oh, we will,' Gideon assured him with husky innuendo, gratified when the older man's humour turned to a frown of concern.

But Gideon's own humour faded once he and Madison were seated in the back of the limousine that would drive them to the film première. Madison sat silently at his side— an unusual enough occurrence; she usually had an answer or something to say about everything!—and she was also chewing distractedly on her bottom lip.

'What's the problem?' Gideon prompted hardly.

'Problem?' she came back sharply, her eyes shimmering silver-green in the half-light from the street lights outside. 'Who said there was a problem?'

He sighed, turning with his arm along the seat behind

her tensed shoulders. 'Okay, so I was wrong earlier to tell you what to wear this evening. Claire was obviously right; you have a better idea of what's suitable than I do.'

Her eyes had widened at his apology, but she looked no less tense because of it.

He let his arm drop about her shoulders. 'Madison—'

'Please don't do that, Gideon,' she snapped, moving away from him to the far side of the leather seat. 'This is business, remember?'

His mouth tightened. 'And it's going to be a complete and utter disaster if you don't lighten up!' he threw back harshly, stung by her obvious aversion to his touch.

He had found his concentration constantly interrupted for the last three weeks by thoughts of this woman, and it annoyed him intensely that she couldn't even stand to have him touch her!

Angry colour heightened the perfection of her cheekbones. 'This was your idea, Gideon, so don't— Oh!' Her indignant gasp was lost as his mouth claimed hers.

He had been hungry for this since the last time he had kissed her, lost in the pleasure of the soft nectar of her lips, of her breasts pressed warmly against his chest as his arms held her locked tightly against him. She was enticing him, filling him with heated desire—

'We're almost there, Mr Byrne,' Jim, the driver, murmured from the front of the limousine.

Gideon moved sharply away from Madison, but not before he had seen the desire that darkened her own eyes— a desire that was quickly hidden as she turned to look out of the window at the crowds of people lining the entrance to the theatre.

Gideon closed his eyes briefly as he too saw those people. Thank goodness Jim had brought him to his senses with that polite reminder of where they were and where they were going—otherwise he would have drawn more attention to himself, and Madison, than even he had planned!

But he had to admire the calmness with which Madison slid gracefully from the back of the limousine as Jim held the door open for them both, straightening to shake back those long, golden tresses, the kiss they had so recently shared adding a glittering sheen to those dark emerald eyes, a flush to her creamy cheeks.

At this moment Madison looked every inch the star Gideon hoped she very soon would be!

It was only as he laced his fingers through hers, prior to walking along the red carpet and into the theatre, that he felt the trembling of her body, and knew she wasn't as composed as she appeared to be...

'You're doing just fine,' he told her softly, even as he smiled for the cameras that were clicking away madly, capturing their appearance here together.

'No thanks to you!' Madison's own smile didn't waver for a moment, that silver-green dress shimmering as she swayed gracefully along at his side, her slender fingers still entwined with his.

He chuckled softly. Claire was right; this woman was more than capable of standing up for herself! 'I only kissed you, Madison; don't make a federal case out of it!' he drawled derisively.

'Then don't repeat it,' she ground out, her eyes flashing with warning.

Oh, he was going to repeat it. Just not for several months. But once he and Madison were no longer working together...!

He felt a shiver of anticipation run through his body.

'Don't tell me you're nervous too, Gideon?' she drawled as she felt that shiver run down his arm into their linked hands.

Certainly not in the way she meant! This sort of thing

meant nothing to him, although, of course, he had a professional interest in seeing the film.

The film world had held a fascination for him ever since he was a child, and in spite of what he had once told Madison he remembered his childhood years in Hollywood very well, and had vowed long ago that he would return there himself in triumph one day. Last year he'd done that, when he'd walked off with the Oscar for Best Director, but with Rosemary he hoped to better even that…

And this woman at his side was going to help him do that!

He turned to give her a bland smile. 'Not at all,' he dismissed coolly.

Madison shrugged. 'Then someone must have been walking over your grave—or jumping up and down on it!' she added with feeling.

Gideon chuckled softly. 'Are you offering to do the deed yourself?' He was aware of the professional smile that continued to curve her lips as they entered the theatre, but he was close enough to see the light of battle in her eyes.

She arched blonde brows. 'To put you there? Or to do the jumping?' she retorted.

His mouth quirked. 'You—'

'Maddie!' A loud greeting interrupted Gideon. 'It is you, isn't it, Madison…?' The question followed that first ecstatic cry of recognition. 'Of course it is.' The man answered his own question dismissively. 'I can't believe it! And I saw Jonny last week, and he didn't say a thing about your being in England. My word, Maddie, you look wonderful!'

Gideon had stiffened defensively as soon as he realised the Maddie in question was, in fact, Madison. Gideon turned slowly to look at the man rapidly approaching, drawing in a sharp breath as he recognised Simon Cauley, the male star of the film they were about to see.

And this man seemed to know Madison well enough to call her an affectionately abbreviated Maddie. He also knew her well enough to tell her how wonderful she looked! And who the hell was Jonny?

But all of those questions went completely out of Gideon's mind as Simon reached Madison's side, sweeping her up off her feet into his arms, even as his mouth came down possessively on hers.

A black tide of rage swept over Gideon, seeming to rob him of all reason, as once again he asked himself, Who the hell *was* Madison McGuire…?

CHAPTER SIX

MADISON pulled back breathlessly, laughing up into Simon's welcoming familiar face; a few minutes ago she had been feeling very uncomfortable and out of place, and Gideon certainly hadn't been helping to alleviate that feeling. 'Put me down, you idiot,' she instructed Simon affectionately. 'People are staring!'

'So what?' he grinned. He was tall and blond, and as handsome as a statue of Apollo. He was also one of the most talented actors Madison had ever seen, and his career had soared into stardom in the last five years. 'I just can't believe you're here.' He shook his head dazedly, smiling his pleasure at the unexpected meeting.

Madison sensed rather than saw the icy displeasure of the man who had brought her here this evening. The man who stood silently at her side. Obviously Gideon did care that people were looking at the three of them with open curiosity!

She gently disengaged herself from Simon's arm, turning to introduce the two men. 'Simon, this is Gideon Byrne. Gideon, Simon—'

'We've already met,' Gideon cut in harshly, shaking the hand the younger man held out to him.

'We even worked together once, a couple of years ago.' Simon nodded lightly, seeming unaware of the other man's coldness.

'So we did,' Gideon acknowledged distantly. 'I wasn't aware the two of you knew each other, though.' He looked at them both with narrowed grey eyes.

'For years,' Simon told him dismissively, still maintaining a hold on one of Madison's hands as he continued to grin at her, his pleasure at seeing her again so obviously genuine. 'Are you coming to the party afterwards?' he pressed Madison eagerly. 'I have to go and do my thing in a moment.' He lightly dismissed the fact that he was the star of the film they were about to sit and watch the première of. 'But I would love to sit and talk with you again later.' He squeezed Madison's hand affectionately. 'Catch up on what's been happening in each other's lives.' He arched blond brows pointedly in Gideon's direction.

Madison turned to look at Gideon too, questioningly, not in the least encouraged by the way in which he included her in that cold look. Well, she couldn't help that; Simon was a long-standing friend, and she certainly wasn't about to be rude to him simply because Gideon looked so annoyed that the two of them were talking together! Besides, she genuinely liked Simon.

'We're leaving straight after watching the film.' Gideon was the one to abruptly answer the other man's question. 'I'm not into celebrity parties,' he added with a scornful grimace.

Simon turned to look at Madison once again. 'How about you, Maddie?' he prompted softly. 'Want to come to a party?'

The coldness emanating from Gideon now was enough to freeze anyone within a two foot radius of him—which literally meant Simon and herself!

Gideon obviously didn't want her to accept the other man's invitation, and as she had come here this evening with Gideon it would be extremely rude of her to go off with another man.

She was well aware she had signed a contract that gave Gideon certain rights over her professional career for the next eight months, but, by the same token, she was not going to have Gideon telling her what she could and couldn't do in her private life…!

'Not tonight, Simon.' She gently turned down the invitation, squeezing his hand in apology. 'But dinner tomorrow evening would be lovely,' she encouraged warmly as she saw his disappointment.

Simon brightened immediately. 'Great! Give me a telephone number where I can reach you,' he said quickly as someone signalled to him across the room.

Madison shook her head regretfully. 'I don't have a pen or paper.' Her bag was only big enough for her lipstick, a hairbrush, and a few notes of money.

Simon took a pen from his inside breast pocket, pulling back the sleeve of his jacket to reveal his shirt cuff. 'Fire away,' he said laughingly.

She shook her head as he scribbled the number she gave him onto the pristine white cuff of his shirt. 'You always were incorrigible!' She laughed disbelievingly.

'See you tomorrow.' Simon bent and gave her a brief kiss on the lips. 'Gideon.' He nodded to the other man before hurrying off to resume his seat.

The silence Simon left behind him was decidedly more uncomfortable than anything Madison had been feeling before that meeting, and a brief look at Gideon from beneath lowered lashes revealed stonily set features and glittering grey eyes.

What on earth was he so damned angry about? Madison wondered, beginning to feel angry herself. What had Gideon expected—that just because he'd only just 'discovered' her she'd lived in seclusion the first twenty-two years of her life, that she knew no one, and consequently no one knew her, either? That wasn't even feasible, let alone believable!

'Gideon—'

'Let's go and find our seats,' he rasped harshly, his grasp on her arm just short of being painful.

Which Madison was sure he knew only too well. He really was annoyed that she knew Simon...

Well, he had no damned right to be! Gideon hadn't given her any choice about accompanying him here this evening, let alone allowed her time or opportunity to tell him she knew the star of the film they were to see!

And the fact that Gideon had kissed her—yet again!— did not give him the right to be rude about her friends.

It had also been nice to see Simon again, she had to admit, smiling to herself as she remembered the fun they had had together in the past. Dinner tomorrow evening promised to be enjoyable.

'How the hell do you know someone like Simon Cauley?'

She turned to look at Gideon as he sternly voiced the question, the two of them walking down the aisle to their seats, Gideon's attendance there obviously causing quite a stir in itself as the audience, of people mainly from the world of film and television, turned to openly look at the two of them with undisguised curiosity.

Madison found that curiosity made her feel a little like a goldfish in a bowl. Didn't that attention bother Gideon? Obviously not, if all he could do was question her about her friendship with Simon!

She gave him a warmly glowing smile—for the benefit of their watching audience; smiling at him was actually the last thing she felt like doing! 'Why shouldn't I know someone like Simon Cauley?' she returned with controlled anger.

Gideon shrugged as they sat down. 'I merely wondered if Simon was the reason you came over to London in need of Edgar's TLC,' he drawled, grey eyes glittering in open challenging as he slowly turned to look at her.

Her eyes flashed angrily as she more than met that challenge, refusing to let her own gaze drop from his. But inside she didn't feel quite so confident. Who on earth had told him she had been in need of tender, loving care when she came over to London? There was only one answer to that— Edgar! For a man successful in business, who was by necessity used to keeping certain things to himself, Edgar seemed to have told Gideon much more about her than she would have wished.

'No, he wasn't,' she snapped, turning pointedly away from him.

'Then perhaps that was Jonny?' Gideon either didn't pick up on the snub or he chose to ignore it.

And Madison knew which one she thought it was! But he obviously thought both Simon and Jonny were past boyfriends of hers—and after the way he had behaved so far this evening she was not in a mood to put him right!

She gave him another saccharine smile. 'No, it wasn't Jonny, either,' she told him huskily.

Gideon's mouth tightened, his gaze raking over her scathingly. 'You certainly get around, don't you?' he bit out insultingly before turning away.

Madison gazed with impotent fury at his stony profile for several seconds before turning away herself. *She* got around! He wasn't exactly an innocent himself, if the gossip columns were to be believed—if only half the stories of his relationships were true, he had no right to cast aspersions on her own behaviour!

Besides which, he was wrong about both Simon and Jonny…Jonny was her brother Jonathan. And he and Simon had been friends from schooldays, which was how Madison came to know Simon too.

Not that she intended telling Gideon any of that; he could think what he liked. The way she felt at the moment, she didn't ever want to talk to him again!

Which was going to be impossible when the two of them were out together for the evening...

However, there was no more opportunity for conversation as the lights went down in the theatre, and Madison's attention was soon caught and held by the plot unfolding on the screen in front of her. Simon, as usual, was outstanding as the hero, and wholly deserved the acclaim he was given at the end of the movie.

Now all Madison had to do was find a way of getting out of here, and back to Edgar's, without giving Gideon the opportunity to insult her enough that she actually ended up hitting him!

She wished now that she had accepted Simon's invitation to join him at the party; at least that way she would have been able to get away from Gideon. But she hadn't, which meant she would have to suffer at least another thirty minutes of Gideon's overbearing company while the limousine drove her home.

She stood silently at Gideon's side, her hand once again gripped firmly in his, as he stopped to talk to several people on their way out, his lack of introduction noticeable to her, as it was to those other people she felt sure. By the time they got outside into the street she was so tense with anger at his deliberate rudeness that her hands were clenched into fists as her sides.

'Mr Byrne,' the driver of their limousine greeted as he opened the door for them to get in.

'Take Miss McGuire back to Remington's, Jim,' Gideon instructed tersely, making no effort to follow Madison into the back of the car.

'Are you not joining us, Mr Byrne?' the driver enquired politely,

'I feel like walking,' Gideon replied sharply, bending down to look inside the car where Madison sat on the back seat. 'Call Claire concerning the details of our travel arrangements on Monday,' he bit out, before straightening, turning on his heel and walking away.

Madison was so taken aback at the suddenness of his departure that she could only sit dazedly in the back of the limousine as the driver closed the door behind her then got back in behind the wheel and drove away. But she recovered enough to turn quickly in her seat to look out the back window, just in time to see Gideon before he disappeared from view around the corner of the street.

Madison slumped back on to the wide leather seat, feeling particularly small and defenceless at this moment. Okay, so she had acknowledged from the beginning that this evening had been business, but it hadn't ever occurred to her that Gideon wouldn't even hang around long enough after the première to see her home! So much for wondering how she was going to politely get rid of him once they got to Edgar's!

She had just been well and truly dumped!

'Whoever she is, guv, she ain't worth it—no woman is!'

Gideon turned wearily to acknowledge with a lift of his hand the call of the Cockney taxi-driver from the open window of his cab as he drove past, his own smile rueful as the man drove on after giving a grin and a wave.

He'd been standing on the middle of the bridge in relative darkness, looking unseeingly down at the murky water moving beneath him, not even sure how he came to have walked here, when the man had called out to him—and it didn't need two guesses what conclusion the taxi-driver had drawn from his actions!

And all the time Gideon had been standing here, not considering taking his own life, but wringing someone else's neck!

Madison McGuire's!

She had been nothing but trouble since he'd first met

her, almost drowning him at their first meeting, falling asleep in his arms from the effect of jet-lag at their second! And as for this evening...!

As Claire had pointed out earlier, he hadn't intended going to this première at all, but after three weeks away in the Isle of Man it had seemed the perfect excuse for him to spend the evening with Madison without it actually appearing as if that was what he wanted to do. And what had happened? Instead of the two of them spending an evening getting to know each other better, as he had planned for them to do, it transpired that Madison was acquainted— well acquainted, it appeared!—with the star of the damned film!

In fact, Madison was becoming such a thorn under his skin that he was coming to rue the day he'd first set eyes on her!

But damn it, he groaned inwardly, it seemed he also couldn't keep his hands off her for any length of time; the curves of her body were driving him crazy, and as for the taste of her lips against his...!

The taxi-driver was right—no woman was worth this agony of confusion. Gideon had decided long ago—while he was still a child, in fact—that no woman would ever mean enough to him that she turned him from his purpose in life. Enjoy women by all means—their company, their humour, their warmth, their lovemaking—but never, ever become emotionally involved with them. That had been his father's downfall, and he had no intention of that ever happening to him!

But Madison, with those emerald eyes he wanted to drown in, that little snub nose with its sprinkling of freckles, that quirky mouth that begged to be kissed, and that body that cried out to be touched, was shaking all his earlier resolves. In fact, he couldn't seem to think straight when he was around her, and wasn't even sure what his resolves were any more.

And as for Simon Cauley kissing her…! The other man was lucky he hadn't just punched him in the mouth, despite their very public surroundings. And those feelings of violence had almost reached breaking point when Madison had suggested having dinner with the other man tomorrow evening! Almost. Because that too had been his father's downfall thirty years ago.

Gideon had only been very young at the time, but he could still remember being told that his father wasn't going to be living with them any more because he had fallen in love with an actress he was working with, that he and Gideon's mother were to be divorced because of the affair.

But it hadn't finished there. In the months that followed his parents' separation the newspapers had been full of stories of his father's rages if anyone should so much as speak about the woman he had fallen in love with. It had affected his career to such an extent that studios had begun to consider he was too much of a publicity risk to employ, and only his staunchest friends, like Edgar and a couple of others, had kept up their friendships with him.

Within a year, it seemed, John Byrne had fallen from grace so dramatically that he was virtually unemployable, taking solace in drink—and the woman he loved, Gideon presumed!—until one night, drunk and angry, he forgot to turn the car wheel at a sharp bend in the road and went straight off the cliff into oblivion.

Gideon had decided then and there that he would never drink alcohol, or love a woman in such a way that he couldn't function without her.

And he hadn't.

He still didn't!

What he felt for Madison wasn't love; it was something else much more basic. Once he had assuaged that physical desire he had for her, he would move on, as he always had in the past. *If* he assuaged that physical desire…

That Madison responded to him he didn't doubt, but he was also aware that she despised herself for doing so. Besides, also because of his father's mistakes, Gideon never became involved with actresses he was actually working with. And, while he refused to become involved, men like Simon Cauley and someone called Jonny were stepping in where he wanted to be.

Hell, he didn't know what he wanted any more. Except that he wanted Madison McGuire with a hunger that was becoming more intense as the days passed…!

One thing he did know for certain: he was not about to let Madison go off to dinner tomorrow evening with Simon Cauley. And luckily, with Madison under contract to appear in his film, he was in a position to ensure it didn't happen…

He turned away from the river with fresh purpose, his step determined as he turned back towards his apartment, a smile of satisfaction curving his lips. Madison was going to be furious when she discovered he'd stepped in and made it impossible for her to see Simon tomorrow evening as planned, and an angry Madison, with those green eyes flashing, was a sight to behold. He felt a warm surge of desire just at the thought of it!

In fact, Gideon's smile turned to a grin of anticipation, his step almost jaunty, as he continued his walk home across the park.

So engrossed was he in his own machiavellian thoughts that he didn't see the man before he stepped out of the darkness of the bushes in front of him, or the bottle he held in his hand before it was raised.

But he did feel the blow as the bottle landed on the side of his head, groaning in protest as he felt his legs give way, before he sank into a dark abyss of nothingness.

CHAPTER SEVEN

'—GETTING out of this damned place!' Madison could hear Gideon announcing arrogantly as she walked down the hospital corridor.

It had taken her almost twenty minutes to get through the hospital security to see him in the first place, and almost another ten minutes to walk along the corridors to the private wing of the hospital where Gideon had apparently been taken after his admission the night before. But by the sound of it he didn't intend being a patient very much longer!

He was standing by the bed pulling on his shirt when Madison let herself into the room she had been told was his. A harassed Claire was standing a little away from him as she obviously tried to talk him out of leaving. From the little Madison knew of Gideon, the other woman might as well save her breath; if he had made up his mind to leave, then that was what he would do.

As he had after the film première the evening before...

It was unbelievable to think that he had actually been mugged after walking away from her so abruptly. At least, Madison had found it unbelievable when told about it earlier, although the gauze square stuck to his right temple seemed to claim otherwise...

His eyes narrowed angrily as he saw her. 'What the hell do you want?' he roared rudely, pulling a jacket on over his shirt, not the dinner suit from last night, but more casual clothes Claire must have brought in with her. 'Come to see how the mighty have fallen?' he added disgustedly.

Madison wasn't in the least disturbed by his obvious displeasure in seeing her here; after last night, she would have been surprised if he had behaved any other way!

She shook her head, smiling slightly. 'I don't see anyone particularly mighty,' she drawled dismissively. 'But from what I understand you did fall…?' She looked at him with brows raised.

His eyes glittered dangerously at her obvious mockery, telling Madison just how much he was hating this! Gideon gave the impression of being completely sufficient unto himself, needing nothing and no one, and to have been attacked in the way he had been, in darkness, by a faceless person, must have really got to him.

He turned accusingly to Claire. 'I suppose you told her I was in here?'

'Not guilty,' Claire assured him with complete honesty, her usual unruffled self—in spite of Gideon's obvious decision to leave before he had actually been discharged by the doctor.

'Actually, it was Uncle Edgar,' Madison informed him mildly. 'He—'

'Does the whole damn world know that I was mugged last night?' Gideon cut in savagely, wincing slightly as the angry contortions of his face obviously caused some discomfort to the injury at his temple.

'I doubt the whole world is interested,' Madison assured him mockingly. 'But Uncle Edgar obviously knows about it, or he wouldn't have been able to tell me,' she reasoned logically.

Gideon shot her a look of intense dislike. 'Well, now that you're here, don't just stand there; you can carry my bag for me!' He strode forcefully from the room without waiting to see whether or not she complied with his order.

Because an order it most certainly was. And Madison was well aware of why he had issued it; Gideon felt a distinct disadvantage at this particular moment, in these circumstances, and the only way he knew how to deal with it was to be as bloody-minded as possible to those close enough to be in the firing line. And at the moment she was a fresh target!

Claire shook her head as she gazed after him. '''Please, Madison. Thank you, Madison'',' she murmured ruefully. 'I'm really sorry about this.' She turned to Madison with genuine regret. 'Perhaps it would have been better if you hadn't come, after all.'

'And missed all the fun?' Madison grinned, shaking her own head as she bent down to pick up the bag that contained Gideon's evening clothes. 'Now that I know Gideon isn't seriously injured—and his temper assures me of that only too well!—I wouldn't have missed this for the world!'

And she wouldn't have. She'd found herself strangely concerned a short time ago when Edgar had told her what had happened to Gideon after he'd left her last night. Strangely, because after the way he had walked off, without even saying goodnight to her, she hadn't particularly cared what happened to him!

But seeing him now, as arrogant and obnoxious as ever, she felt completely reassured as to his complete recovery from whatever injuries he had suffered. Although she had a feeling it was his pride that had taken the biggest blow...

Claire chuckled softly. 'He is rather like a bear with a sore head, isn't he?'

'A *Gideon* with a sore head—which is worse!' she corrected her laughingly. 'Come on, let's go and see how far he got; it was like trying to get into Fort Knox to get in, so it must be even more difficult to get out!'

They caught up with Gideon at the reception to the private wing, in the process of signing his own discharge papers, the nurse giving the two of them a pitying look over the top of his bent head, as if to say, How do you put up with this man all the time?

To Madison's relief, she didn't have to, and she knew that Claire took absolutely no notice of Gideon's mercurial moods, that the other woman was more than capable of taking care of herself in any of their verbal exchanges.

He pushed the papers back towards the nurse, straightening to shoot the two waiting women an impatient glance before striding out of the hospital. Again without waiting to see if they followed him.

'I guess my date this evening was just cancelled,' Claire muttered to Madison as they strolled outside, looking down ruefully at the black dress and red jacket she was obviously wearing in preparation for going on to that date after visiting Gideon.

'Not at all,' Madison assured her lightly as she watched Gideon signal a taxi from the waiting rank. 'Gideon is only in need of a verbal punch-bag for the next couple of hours; he can damn well make do with me!' She didn't see why he should be allowed to ruin the other woman's plans for the evening just because he'd chosen to discharge himself from hospital.

Claire grimaced at this suggestion. 'That doesn't seem very fair to you,' she said hesitantly.

Madison squeezed her arm reassuringly. 'Believe me, I can handle it.'

Claire looked skeptical. 'He can get worse than this, you know.' She pulled another face.

Madison laughed softly. 'I'm not sure I would recognise him any other way! Look, don't worry about it.' She gave the other woman's arm another comforting squeeze. 'Get in another taxi.' She indicated several empty ones waiting for fares. 'Go off and enjoy your evening. And leave Gideon to me,' she added determinedly, giving Gideon a narrow-eyed look where he had got into the back of the taxi.

'Thanks,' Claire grinned at her. 'You'll get your reward one day!' She hurried off to get into another of the taxis.

Madison took her time joining Gideon, putting his bag in the boot of the car before getting in beside him, although she was aware all the time of the fact that he had watched Claire drive off in another vehicle...

'You drew the short straw, did you?' he demanded, turning to look at her accusingly in the relative darkness.

She shrugged, settling back in the seat as the car pulled away. 'Claire has a date.'

'Unless I'm mistaken, so do you,' he bit out coldly.

And he was very rarely mistaken! But in this case he was, by several hours. Simon had telephoned her, as planned, but after considering the fact of her early start for the Isle of Man in the morning Madison had thought it better if they had lunch together rather than dinner; a late night tonight would not be conducive to traveling with Gideon early tomorrow!

At the time she'd had no idea Gideon was in hospital, or that several hours later she would be visiting him there!

'With Simon Cauley,' Gideon added derisively when Madison's answer wasn't immediately forthcoming.

'The film was good last night, wasn't it?' she said admiringly.

He nodded tersely. 'More than good,' he acknowledged economically. 'But I'm sure Cauley doesn't need us to tell him that!'

She most certainly had told Simon that earlier today! In fact, they had spent a very enjoyable couple of hours together. At least she could relax in Simon's company—something she found impossible to do when with Gideon!

She shrugged again. 'Everyone needs a little praise sometimes.' Except Gideon, of course; *he* already knew he was brilliant!

'So why aren't you out giving Cauley his?' Gideon scorned.

For some reason she felt reluctant to tell him she and Simon had already met for lunch, probably because of that scornful attitude Gideon seemed to have adopted whenever he talked of the other man. Whatever the reason, she was not about to tell him anything about her lunch with Simon...

'I'm sure you should be taking things easy, Gideon,' she told him briskly. 'With no unnecessary excitement.'

His mouth twisted derisively. 'Talking of Simon Cauley does not cause me any excitement!'

But it didn't soothe his temper any, either!

'But maybe you were referring to yourself when you made that last comment,' he added insultingly.

Madison drew in a sharp breath. He really was the most aggravating, insulting man she had ever met! 'Not particularly, Gideon,' she drawled unconcernedly. 'Now, what did the hospital say about your after-care?'

'Damn what the hospital says!' he exploded furiously. 'I'm thirty-eight years old; I'll do what I damn well please!'

'What's new?' she bit out caustically, turning to look unseeingly out of the window, effectively cutting off their conversation with her obvious lack of interest in anything else he had to say.

She wished she had never gone to the hospital in the first place, had no real idea why she had done so. Except that it had seemed like the right thing to do at the time, and Uncle Edgar had agreed with her when she'd told him what she intended doing. For all the gratitude Gideon showed she might just as well have stayed at home and done her packing!

'Don't tell me you were offering to sit at my bedside and mop my fevered brow?' Gideon cut mockingly into her indignant thoughts.

'Only if it was with a freezing cold ice-pack!' she snapped. 'You really are the most ungrateful swine I've ever met, Gideon.' She rounded on him furiously. 'Claire obviously took time out of her own evening tonight to bring your clothes in to you, and all you could do was be rude to her. And—'

'You've done the same thing, and I'm being equally rude to you,' he conceded ruefully, that angry edge gone from his voice now. 'Would it help if I said I was sorry?' he added huskily.

Madison stared at him. Gideon had just apologised. And she had once inwardly accused him of being a man who never apologised for anything he did or said!

He laughed softly at her dazed expression. 'I'm not really that uncompromising, am I?'

'Worse!' she confirmed with feeling.

He quirked dark brows. 'I did say I was sorry.'

'I'm sure Claire will be glad to hear it—'

'I wasn't apologising to Claire,' he murmured huskily.

He suddenly seemed very close to her in the back of the car, Madison held mesmerised by the silver glitter of his eyes. He really did have the most beautiful eyes, and his lashes were—

'Not again, Gideon!' She straightened self-consciously, moving determinedly away from him. 'You seem to make a habit of kissing me in the back of cars!' she explained abruptly at his questioning look. 'Something I grew out of when I left senior school!'

He continued to look at her for several long seconds, and then his mouth twisted derisively. 'I'm sorry to disappoint you, Madison,' he drawled tauntingly, 'but I was not about to kiss you. I have slightly blurred vision since my knock on the head last night,' he continued mockingly. 'I was merely endeavouring to put you into focus. My only consolation is that if you think *I* look bad you should see the other guy!' he added with satisfaction.

She had been sure he was about to kiss her! Or was it just that, for a very brief moment, she had wanted to be kissed…?

No!

She couldn't deny, to herself at least, that she responded when Gideon kissed her, but she couldn't actually be falling for him, could she? Not Gideon Byrne. That wasn't the real reason she'd felt compelled to come to the hospital this evening once she'd learnt of his injury, was it?

It would be like falling in love with a chameleon; she never knew from one moment to the next what he was going to do or say!

But some people would say that was better than boredom…

They might do, but they weren't the ones who would have to live with such an impossible love. Because Gideon had made it more than obvious he didn't intend falling in love with anyone!

She'd come to London to recover from the disappointment of one love affair; she simply couldn't fall in love with a man as unreachable as Gideon.

She couldn't.

She *mustn't*!

'The other guy?' Madison prompted distantly beside him just when he'd decided she wasn't going to speak again.

Gideon nodded. 'I regained consciousness as he was going through my pockets; I believe he was admitted to hospital last night too!'

It had been the shock of Gideon's life to regain consciousness and realise he was being mugged, and he had reacted instinctively, knocking the other man to the ground, breaking his jaw in the process—so he'd been informed by the policeman who'd visited him in his hospital room late last night so that he could take his statement about the incident.

He looked at Madison searchingly as she remained silent after his explanation, noticing how pale she'd suddenly become. 'I'm not a lover of violence, either, Madison,' he asserted harshly. 'But neither am I about to let someone just knock me out and try to rob me!'

'Of course not,' she acknowledged quietly.

He frowned across at her. 'You don't sound very convinced?'

'What do you want me to say, Gideon?' She sighed wearily. 'As I understand it, the man actually hit you with a bottle; of course you had to defend yourself.'

Then why was it he had just felt the need to justify his actions?

He'd felt so damned annoyed earlier when he'd turned and found Madison in his hospital room; it was the last place he would have wanted her to see him, especially under such circumstances. But his annoyance had abated somewhat once he realised that, instead of going out to dinner with Simon Cauley this evening, Madison was actually accompanying him home to his apartment.

But her lack of conviction just now concerning his defensive behaviour the previous evening irritated him all over again! With the rage that had engulfed Gideon last night when he'd realised exactly what was going on, the man was lucky he had got away with just a broken jaw!

But perhaps it was something else that was bothering Madison...

'It isn't going to affect our travel plans for tomorrow, you know,' he assured her softly. 'You may have to lead me about by the arm for a few days, but I'm sure the vision will clear eventually!' he added self-derisively.

Madison merely nodded distractedly, confirming that she

wasn't really listening to what he was saying. What the hell was wrong with her?

'Claire brought the newspapers in earlier,' he told her lightly. 'The première, Madison; you do remember we went to one last night?' he prompted in response to her blank look.

Gideon could only feel relief that they'd finally reached his apartment block, getting out to pay the driver, turning to find Madison standing at his side, his bag in her hand. He supposed he should feel grateful that, after seeing him safely delivered to his home, she hadn't decided to just stay in the taxi and continue on to Edgar's apartment!

Except he didn't feel very grateful. Somewhere back in the conversation he'd lost Madison—and he had no idea where or why!

He was more than ever aware of Madison's silence as they came up in the lift and walked down the corridor to his apartment. He unlocked the door to switch on the lights before turning to look at her. 'What's wrong, Madison?' He grasped her by the shoulders, looking down at her with narrowed eyes, filled with impatience as she avoided meeting his gaze.

'Nothing,' she dismissed tersely, looking everywhere but at him. 'Can I get you a cup of tea or coffee?' she offered, frowning.

This was the last place she wanted to be; Gideon was more and more convinced of that as the seconds passed. But, perversely, this was exactly where he wanted her to be!

'Coffee would be fine,' he accepted, releasing her. 'I'll get the newspapers out of my bag so that you can have a look at them when you come back.'

It took him all of thirty seconds to locate the newspapers and put them on the low coffee-table in front of the sofa, and the other three or four minutes it took for Madison to make the coffee he spent going back over their conversation in the car to see if he could pin-point what it was he had said or done this time to upset her.

And she was upset, he acknowledged. Usually she was angry with him for one thing or another, and that anger he could deal with; she just looked more kissable than ever with her green eyes flashing and her cheeks flushed.

Kissable...

Maybe that was it? She had thought he was about to kiss her in the car—and she had been right, of course!—and he had teased her into thinking he never intended doing any such thing. But what was he supposed to do? She'd just very clearly told him not to even attempt to kiss her; of course he was going to deny the intention!

But could that be the reason why she had suddenly become uncharacteristically quiet...?

He looked up as she came back into the room with the coffee. *Two* steaming mugs of it, Gideon noted with satisfaction, so she didn't intend leaving immediately.

He made room on the table for the mugs, picking up one of the newspapers to show her the page of photographs that had been taken at the première the previous evening. There was a rather good one of the two of them together right in the middle of the page.

'''Gideon Byrne and mystery friend''...?' She read the caption beneath the photograph, having sat down beside him on the sofa—although far enough away so that no part of them touched, he noted ruefully. Even accidentally!

She shook her head. 'I still don't understand this.' She indicated the newspaper. 'That clause in my contract—'

'Has nothing to do with last night. It was done under my control,' he explained at her puzzled look. 'And don't worry,' he drawled. 'You won't remain a mystery for too much longer!'

She abruptly put the newspaper back down on the table. 'I'm not worrying,' she bit out dismissively.

Gideon shook his head. 'Something is bothering you,' he said slowly. 'Did I say or do anything earlier to offend you?'

She gave a rueful smile. 'When didn't you?'

'A natural ability I have where you're concerned, hmm?' He grimaced self-derisively.

'Something like that,' she said with a sigh, picking up her mug to begin drinking the hot coffee, almost burying her face in the cup.

Gideon wasn't used to situations like this. His intimate relationships with women were all based on no pressure, no demands, and when the relationship stopped being fun any more he ended it. And temperamental actresses he could deal with too, and had done so, on several occasions. But Madison was neither of those two things; there was no intimate relationship between them, and he hadn't actually become her director yet.

'Have you argued with Cauley?' he probed frowningly.

'Of course not!' she denied incredulously. 'Simon and I have been friends for years; it isn't the sort of friendship that has the sort of arguments you're talking about.'

Then what sort of friendship was it, damn it? No matter which way he approached the subject of the other man, Madison blocked answering his questions in any outright manner. And it was really starting to get to him.

But then, of course, she *was* twenty-two years old, and as such would have had relationships; he just didn't like the idea of Simon Cauley being one of them. Not only was the other man the male lead of the moment, much in demand by directors, with work lined up for years ahead, but he was also a hell of a nice man. He was also single, very eligible, and had an easy familiarity with Madison that drove Gideon crazy!

She stood up abruptly. 'I think I'd better go, Gideon—'

'And I think you hadn't!' he grated, standing up too. 'Madison, I don't know what's happening here—any more than I think you do—but I do know that our efforts to squash it are just making us both miserable!'

He'd said far more than he meant to say, and he could see by Madison's startled expression that she wished he hadn't said it either. But it was too late for that; the words had been said, and somehow they were going to have to come to some sort of understanding so that the two of them could work together for the next eight months.

She swallowed hard, shaking her head. 'Gideon—'

He couldn't stand it any more. He did what he had wanted to do since they'd parted so abruptly the previous evening. He pulled her into his arms, moulding her body close against his, and his mouth came down possessively on hers.

So much for his decision the evening before, as he'd stared down at the murky depths of the river, that he had to keep a physical distance between himself and Madison!

CHAPTER EIGHT

IT WAS as if the time that had elapsed since she had last been in Gideon's arms had never happened. There was no gentle build-up to their passion but a continuation of that explosion, the two of them hungry for each other, mouths and hands searching, the buttons on Madison's blouse no obstacle to Gideon as he pushed the garments impatiently aside, his lips now against the creamy softness of her skin.

Madison's throat arched at the feel of his hotly possessive mouth, one of his hands lightly cupping her breast through the silky material of her bra as his lips sought the throbbing tip, the moan low in her throat as he found it, hot pleasure coursing through her body at the moist caress of his tongue against her roused flesh.

Her fingers caressed and then clung on to the broad width of his shoulders, a fierce fire engulfing her thighs as she felt the pulse of his desire there, lids closed over eyes dark with her own desire.

And then the silky barrier of her bra was no longer between them either, Madison feeling her legs give way beneath her as her pouting nipple was taken into Gideon's mouth, offering no protest as she was swung up into his arms to be laid gently down on the sofa they had so recently sat on side by side. He joined her there and they lay close together, his lips and hands feasting on the nakedness of her breasts.

Madison's fingers were entwined in the dark thickness of his hair as she held him to her, her legs entangled with his as she sought closer contact still, breathing heavily in

110

her arousal, her body filled with a restless need that she knew Gideon could assuage.

'You're beautiful, Madison,' Gideon groaned huskily, having discarded his own shirt now, their heated skin searing against each other. 'Absolutely, perfectly beautiful!'

So was he, his chest darkly tanned, the hair that grew there silky soft against her sensitised skin. And she knew that the rest of him would be just as physically perfect and arousing.

She let out a satisfied sigh as his lips claimed hers once again, enjoying the weight of him as he moved so that he lay above her, the movement of his body against hers asserting his need to make love to her.

Their lips sipped and tasted, and then sipped again, Gideon's tongue moving erotically across her parted lips before plunging into the moistness inside.

Madison felt utterly claimed by him, knew herself to be totally desired, groaning as she felt herself floating in a sea of physical need, all control lost, her whole body becoming suffused with a warmth that shuddered through every particle of her.

Pleasure, like nothing she'd ever known before, swept through her entire body like a tidal wave, carrying her along in its flow, until finally she lay back weak but exhilarated.

Gideon raised his head to look at her with almost black eyes. 'Madison...?'

She couldn't believe what had just happened to her. Internal combustion. And of a kind completely created by Gideon...!

But as she looked up at him she was filled with a shyness that made her quickly avert her gaze. What was she doing? What had she just done?

'Don't turn away from me,' he said throatily, his hand gently touching her cheek as he turned her face back towards him. 'Madison, I—'

'Please don't, Gideon,' she burst out forcefully, fully aware now of their half-nakedness—and of what she had just experienced. And it was like nothing she had ever known before. How much more physically consuming it would be if Gideon fully made love to her!

But he mustn't do that. They couldn't do that. It would make the next months impossible, a sheer torture.

What she had just felt with Gideon made a nonsense of her past relationships, but especially the one with Gerry. That relationship, in all their weeks together, had never reached this physical level. And despite the hunger she still felt for Gideon, the knowledge that there was even more than what she had already experienced, she knew this had to stop.

Now.

For both their sakes.

She pulled away from him to sit up, pulling her blouse back on over her nakedness, doing the buttons back up with fingers that still shook slightly. 'I'm sure this doesn't rate as "mopping your fevered brow",' she told him self-derisively, standing up to thrust her bra into her shoulder-bag before running her moist hands down her denim-clad thighs.

There was something particularly unpleasant about picking up your own clothes from the floor where they had been thrown uncaringly in the midst of passion a few minutes earlier!

'You do realise this was a mistake?' She still couldn't quite look at him, her gaze focusing somewhere over his left shoulder.

He shrugged. 'I've made a few in my time,' he murmured huskily.

She smiled humourlessly. 'This probably ranks up there with some of the bigger ones!' She sighed heavily. 'I suggest we try to forget—'

'That it ever happened?' Gideon cut in harshly, pulling on his shirt now as he sat up on the sofa. 'I think that's pushing credibility too far!' He shook his head, his expression grim. 'I know damn well I can't forget it—do you think you can?'

Of course she couldn't—but she could act as if she had! After all, she was an actress—wasn't she...? It was the only part of her, until this evening, that she had thought Gideon was interested in.

She *still* thought it. Okay, so they were attracted to each other, had a physical effect on each other that was explosive. But on Gideon's part that was all it was—physical. He had no intention of falling in love with her.

Whereas for her it was too late. She already loved him.

She had suspected as much in the car earlier, but she was utterly convinced of it now. And she couldn't have chosen someone more emotionally unreachable than Gideon. Oh, if she were agreeable they could probably have an affair for several months—probably for the duration of their working together—but ultimately Gideon would end it. As he obviously had all his previous relationships. And she would end up more broken-hearted than she was now.

No, better to put an end to it now. Whatever 'it' was!

'I think it best if I leave now, Gideon,' she began softly, still not quite looking at him.

'So you intend seeing Cauley this evening?' he asked harshly, a cold edge to his voice now.

She had no intention of seeing Simon tonight, and under different circumstances she would have told Gideon exactly why not. But her friendship with the younger man obviously annoyed him, and an annoyed Gideon was easier for her to deal with than the physically arousing one of a few short minutes ago. Besides, she had to get out of here with some of her pride left intact!

She glanced at her wristwatch. 'It's only nine o'clock.

And, as I'm sure you're well aware, actors and actresses are usually night people.' She didn't actually answer his question; lying wasn't something she did too easily, nor was it something she particularly enjoyed. But evasion, she felt, was perfectly acceptable!

Gideon turned away abruptly. 'Then you'd better not let me keep you,' he ground out. 'I'll see you at the airport at eight-thirty in the morning. The plane leaves at nine-thirty.'

Back to business, Madison acknowledged ruefully. But what else had she expected? Gideon was a film director first and foremost, and nothing—as she was learning to her emotional cost—was ever allowed to interfere with that.

She wished she could be as emotionally compartmental, put all of her emotions into neat little boxes, to be taken out when the right situation presented itself. But she simply wasn't like that; she knew that her feelings for Gideon were going to cause her a lot of pain and heartache over the next few months.

She needed until eight-thirty in the morning to come to terms with that. If she ever did!

'Eight-thirty.' She nodded in confirmation. 'I'll see myself out, shall I?' she murmured ruefully as he made no effort to get up off the sofa.

Gideon looked at her coldly. 'Why not? You saw yourself in!' he dismissed harshly.

That wasn't strictly true, although admittedly she'd arrived at the hospital earlier uninvited. And that earlier concern she'd felt for his welfare now seemed a complete waste of time; Gideon needed no one, and he certainly didn't want anyone needing him either. She didn't *need* him; she simply loved him…!

Although, she decided somewhat desolately on the ride home in the taxi, there was nothing simple about loving Gideon. He was the most complex man she had ever met.

It was just her misfortune that she had fallen in love with him!

Madison let herself quietly into the apartment when she got back, hoping not to alert Edgar to the fact that she was home. He was sure to ask how her visit to Gideon had gone, and at the moment she just didn't feel up to answering his questions about the other man. In fact, she was more likely to burst out crying if Edgar so much as mentioned Gideon's name!

She almost made it, too; the lounge was empty, and the kitchen when she went in there to get herself a glass of water. It was only as she walked softly down the hallway to the guest bedroom that Edgar's bedroom door suddenly opened and he came out into the hallway, tying the belt to his dressing-gown as he did so.

Madison looked at him almost guiltily, feeling as if the passion she had just shared with Gideon was emblazoned across her face. But as she reluctantly met Edgar's gaze she found he was the one who looked slightly uncomfortable.

It was only nine-thirty at night. And in all the time she had been staying here she had never known Edgar to go to bed before eleven o'clock, usually nearer midnight. And, from his bare legs and feet, he didn't look as if he was wearing anything under his dressing-gown…

Oops!

'I wasn't expecting you back just yet,' he told her awkwardly.

That very awkwardness confirmed for Madison that she was probably right in thinking Edgar wasn't alone in his bedroom! Poor man; it was his apartment, after all, and she had been staying here for weeks. And the first real opportunity he'd found to be alone with his latest girlfriend, and she had come home early and interrupted them!

'I'm going straight to bed,' she assured him hastily. 'I need an early night.' How embarrassing! For all of them.

'Of course, but— Your mother called,' Edgar remembered with a frown.

'Did she…?' Madison wasn't encouraged by that frown.

He nodded, his brows raised questioningly. 'She would like you to call her back.'

Not *now*. She couldn't talk to her mother now. Her mother would know, just from the tone of her voice, that something was wrong; her mother was the one person she'd never been able to fool by her acting! And if she thought there was something wrong she would be on the next plane over here. Only to find Madison was no longer in London…

'I'll call her from the island,' Madison promised. 'Now you get back to—bed,' she finished, with a lame grimace for the awkwardness of the situation they both found themselves in, although neither of them had actually voiced the reason for it. 'And don't bother to get up and see me off in the morning. Claire is calling for me at seven-thirty, so there's really no point.' And it would mean Edgar didn't have to disturb his morning—or anything else!

'Fine.' Edgar nodded tersely. 'But you won't forget to call your mother, will you? You know what she's like,' he added pointedly.

Oh, yes, she knew all too well what her mother was like. But it wasn't going to be easy avoiding answering her direct questions.

Just as it wasn't going to be easy facing Gideon tomorrow morning…!

Gideon sat back in his seat on the plane, his eyes closed, on the pretext that his vision was no longer blurred, but that he now had a headache. But he wasn't asleep. Just as he hadn't slept last night after Madison had left him so abruptly. To go and spend what was left of the evening with Simon Cauley. Possibly the night, too…!

She was looking at him now. He didn't need to open his eyes, or turn his head to look across the aisle where she sat near the window next to Claire, to know that she was giving him another of those apprehensive glances. She had been looking at him in that way since she'd arrived at the airport earlier with Claire, as if she half expected to feel the lash of contempt from his tongue or gaze at any moment—and she intended being prepared for it if it should happen!

The truth of the matter was, he didn't quite know how to deal with her at the moment. Last night he'd been so damned angry with her he could quite cheerfully have strangled her when she told him she was leaving him to go straight to Cauley.

She'd been like fire in his arms last night, and there was no way she could ever deny her response to him. But she had still left him and gone to another man!

And so this morning, when she'd arrived at the airport with Claire, he had merely nodded a terse greeting to her. Because he didn't trust himself to speak to her!

What was there to say? What could he say? He'd broken his own rule again last night, and was having enough trouble dealing with that, without having to deal with Madison's moods. They had to find some level on which they could work together—and at the moment he couldn't see what the hell it was going to be!

He shouldn't have kissed her. And he most certainly shouldn't have touched her. Except that he had enjoyed doing both those things more than he had ever enjoyed anything else in his life...! Madison tasted of cream and honey, and her skin felt like silk—smooth, flowing, responsive silk. He still ached from the need he had felt for her last night!

Thoughts like this weren't going to help him get through the next few months!

'—landing, Gideon.' One of Claire's hands was placed on his arm to accompany her words.

He turned to look at her blankly, realising as he did so that the announcement to put seat belts on because they were landing must have been made—and he hadn't heard a word of it. Damn it, this had to stop, he chided himself as he impatiently refastened his seat belt. He had a film to make, and Madison was its star.

Madison…!

'Yes?' She was looking across at him with wildly startled eyes.

He had spoken her name out loud! Hell, he was acting like some besotted schoolboy. And he was neither of those things. And although he was attracted to Madison—there was no denying that—he most certainly wasn't in love with her. He had never been in love with any of the women he had ever been involved with.

'Have you fastened your seat belt?' he rapped out.

She looked dazed. 'Of course.'

He nodded. 'What do you think of the island so far?' he prompted; the plane was now flying along its eastern coastline, bound for the airport at the south of the island.

She frowned, as if she hadn't even been aware they were near the island. 'It looks very pretty,' she finally said with dismissive generality.

It *was* a pretty island. It also had stretches of the unspoilt, rugged coastline that were necessary for the opening scenes of the film, and the rolling countryside that was necessary for the scenes of Rosemary's maturity. They had even found the ideal manor house that could be used for filming as Rosemary's home. Yes, the Isle of Man was the perfect setting for his film.

But it must look very small and rural to a girl brought up in the States, in Nevada, of all places, with her family involved in the running of casinos…

He nodded impatiently, turning away. A discontented star could be a problem he hadn't even begun to think about. Until now. Hell, Madison McGuire was becoming more trouble than even he could have imagined.

Although she looked happy enough as she sat in the back of the car next to Claire on the way from the airport, looking out at the late spring scenery of the island—the gorse in deep yellow bloom along the roadside, bright splashes of flowers: bluebells, white bells, a few late daffodils. The sun was shining down on the aprons of fields, some arable, others for grazing sheep and cattle.

'Say hello to the fairies,' the driver instructed lightly as they went over a small white bridge aptly named the Fairy Bridge, putting up his hand in familiar greeting.

'It's bad luck if you don't,' Claire told Madison as she raised her own hand and murmured a greeting.

'Claire is Manx, and slightly superstitious with it,' Gideon supplied dryly as he raised his hand. Madison looked slightly dazed by their behaviour.

'How wonderful!' She turned to look back at the bridge, her face alight with pleasure.

Gideon felt an ache in his chest at that smile on her face. She never looked at him like that!

'Head hurting again, Gideon?' Claire was frowning at him.

Because he had been frowning himself, he realised irritably. 'A little,' he dismissed noncommittally, turning back to the scenery in front of him.

He could hear the two women talking in the back of the car as Madison asked Claire questions about the island where she had been born but left several years ago to further her career. But Gideon didn't join in their conversation, not wanting to look at Madison for the moment.

This was a living hell. Every time Madison so much as

smiled at anyone or anything else, he felt angry that the smile wasn't for him. What the hell did that mean?

'Could the two of you keep the noise down?' he rasped at the two women without turning. 'You're making my head ache with your inane chatter!' And his head did ache, in fact it throbbed, but that was the consequence of his own troubled thoughts.

Nevertheless, the two women lowered their voices as they continued to talk, so much so that he could no longer hear what they were saying. And that annoyed him too.

Everything annoyed him at the moment. And Madison McGuire most of all.

Or was it just these unfathomable feelings he had towards her that were causing that…?

Whatever the reason, he'd never felt so disgruntled and out of sorts with everything, and everyone, in his life before! And he knew he wasn't the easiest tempered man at the best of times.

Douglas, the capital of the island, with its thriving financial sector, was a prosperous as well as pretty town, and obviously came as something of a surprise to Madison as she quietly asked Claire questions about the place while the car drove along the promenade and out along the scenic coastal road.

It even irritated him that Madison and Claire seemed to get along so well together. It was part of what Claire was paid to do, and yet with Madison the friendship seemed to have passed well beyond Claire's job description.

Was he the only one that Madison seemed to annoy without even trying? It would seem so. So perhaps he was the one with the problem?

He felt relieved when they reached the house they were renting for their approximate two months' stay on the island, requesting the driver to wait while he saw the two women and their luggage inside the house, as he intended to go back out again to meet his camera crew who should still have been hard at work even in his absence. Besides, he needed to get away from Madison McGuire for a while.

'Choose any of the bedrooms except the one to the right at the top of the stairs,' he instructed abruptly, throwing the keys to the house down on the kitchen table. 'Unless you want to share,' he added dryly, his expression hard as he finally looked at Madison.

She looked glorious, her hair cascading down her back, her face appearing free of make-up, but more beautiful because of that, her green eyes darkly troubled now as she met his gaze. Damn it. It was just what he hadn't wanted—a female star who was so wary of him she couldn't even relax, let alone act!

'With you?' Claire tauntingly took up the conversation. 'No, thanks, Gideon,' she assured him.

His mouth twisted. 'How about you, Madison? We could keep each other warm at night.'

Claire turned slowly to give him a narrow-eyed look. And she was perfectly justified in her disapproval; she knew as well as he did that he wasn't serious about the invitation.

At least, he hoped he wasn't...

'Unless I'm mistaken, this house has central heating,' Madison came back hardly.

'But Nevada must be quite a warm place to live?' he persisted.

'But I haven't lived there for some time,' she reminded him defensively.

Gideon knew he had taken this joke quite far enough, if any of them considered it as such, and yet some devil inside him kept pushing him on. 'Exactly where did you live before you came to stay with Uncle Edgar?' he prompted tauntingly.

Madison's eyes narrowed. 'Where—or who with?'

He shrugged, the tension icy between them now. 'Whatever.'

'New York,' she told him flatly. 'And it's very cold there in the winter months; I'm sure I'll manage just fine here. But thanks for the offer.' She met his gaze unflinchingly.

'Okay,' he nodded sternly, tired of the subject himself now. 'The two of you get settled in; I'll be back later.'

'Er, Gideon…?' Claire halted him at the door. 'What do we do about food?' she asked as he turned back impatiently.

'Try looking in the fridge,' he replied, making good his escape this time.

Because escape it most certainly was.

And all because of Madison McGuire!

She might respond to him—in fact he knew to his own cost, and a sleepless night, just how she responded to him!—but it had become more and more apparent to him, as today had progressed, that Madison didn't particularly *like* him…!

CHAPTER NINE

'HE HATES me!' Madison groaned as she dropped down on to one of the chairs around the kitchen table, her face buried in her hands.

'I don't think so,' Claire disagreed lightly, moving about the kitchen checking on the supplies Gideon said had been left there for their arrival. 'Gideon never stirs himself enough emotionally to feel so strongly for anyone!' she stated bluntly.

Gideon had been stirred enough emotionally last night, but it hadn't been with the gentle emotion of love but with passion, as Madison knew only too well. Facing him again at the airport this morning had been one of the hardest things she had ever had to do, and Gideon, with his long silences, hadn't made it any easier for her. And his mockery just now about the two of them sharing a room here had only added to the pain of loving him.

She still wasn't quite sure how that had happened, and had decided in the end that it didn't matter how it had happened—she just did! And Gideon was about as easy to love as a porcupine; he had so many prickly barbs sticking out of him; it was impossible to get close to him in the ordinary way of things.

And what had happened between them last night must never be repeated. As it was, the two of them could hardly bear to look at each other—Madison because she loved him, and Gideon because—well, because no matter what Claire might think to the contrary, Gideon could stir himself enough for intense anger. And he'd been furious at her ever since what had happened between them last night!

'Hey.' Claire came and sat down at the kitchen table with her, looking searchingly at Madison now as she lightly touched her arm. 'What is it, Madison?' she prompted with concern. 'Did something happen between you and Gideon last night?' she guessed shrewdly.

She liked Claire, knew she had found a friend in the other woman, but she wasn't ready to share her feelings for Gideon with anyone. Besides, she half suspected— Well, never mind what she suspected; it was none of her business, anyway…

She grimaced. 'Nothing worth talking about,' she dismissed, not quite able to meet the other woman's gaze. 'But you heard him just now; the man is impossible!' She shook her head with feeling.

Claire laughed softly. 'I told you, the trick with Gideon is never let him know he's getting to you. Because if you do he'll make your life hell!'

Madison sighed. 'I don't know how you put up with him.'

'Well…there is a second thing about Gideon that perhaps I should have mentioned,' Claire said. 'Don't get emotionally involved with him yourself; you'll just end up getting hurt.'

The warning came far too late for Madison. And both women knew it.

Although as they unpacked in the bedrooms they had chosen for their own—both of them studiously ignoring the bedroom they knew to be Gideon's—and then prepared lunch together, neither of them mentioned the subject again.

Madison did find it odd, after having a good look round, that there appeared to be no one else but the three of them staying in this rather large house. All the other bedrooms were obviously empty.

'Gideon likes plenty of room,' Claire explained when Madison mentioned this fact.

Madison's mouth twisted ruefully. 'And I'm sure it has nothing at all to do with Clause 27 in my contract!' She quirked knowing brows at the other woman.

'Now, I didn't say that…' Claire acknowledged dryly.

'Because we both know our seclusion here has everything to do with that!' Madison said disgustedly. And she didn't particularly relish being alone here with Gideon, even with Claire present!

'Stop worrying so much,' the other woman chided. 'I can assure you , this is much more comfortable accommodation than the rest of the cast have!'

She wasn't concerned with the comfort; it was being virtually alone here with Gideon that bothered her.

'Come on.' Claire stood up, the two of them having cleared away from lunch. 'Gideon has left the car here, so I can take you for a drive around the island.'

Madison hesitated. 'What if Gideon should come back and find us gone?' He hadn't said he would need her at all today, but then he hadn't said he wouldn't either…

Claire shrugged. 'So what if he does? I really can't see the point of the two of us just sitting here waiting for him to come back; he could be hours.'

And Madison didn't particularly want to be here when he did come back. Besides, it was a lovely day; they might as well go out and enjoy it.

It was impossible not to enjoy herself as Claire acted as her driver and guide for the afternoon. She was amazed there were so many differing terrains on such a small island, with hills and valleys, plus moorland, the capital town of Douglas, and the city of Peel, with its cathedral.

'It's like miniature England,' Madison realised admiringly.

'But better,' Claire told her firmly. 'Of course, I'm prejudiced, but I think it's much nicer than England. I've always thought our ways are about twenty-five years behind

England. And, of course, because there's simply nowhere to run, the island doesn't have the everyday crime that the mainland has, or indeed places like the States,' she added thoughtfully.

Madison found it very endearing the way the sophisticated Claire had reverted to defending her Manx origins. And it seemed the other woman's surname, Christian, was also very Manx—probably the most well-known person in history with that name had been Fletcher Christian, a descendant of a family originally from the Isle of Man. Although Claire seemed to think the connection wasn't a particularly attractive one, considering the man had been notorious for inciting the mutiny on the ship the *Bounty*!

'I've seen the movie!' Madison laughed teasingly.

Claire smiled too. 'Don't believe everything you see on the big screen! For one thing, I doubt the real Fletcher Christian was anywhere near as gorgeous as Marlon Brando was when he made that particular film! And if history is to be believed the mutineers made a complete mess of things after throwing Captain Bligh and some of the crew off the ship and "sailing off into the sunset"—so much so that, after burning the *Bounty*, they eventually destroyed each other on Pitcairn Island. Don't look so surprised.' Claire laughed as Madison looked amused by her jaundiced account. 'As a probable distant relation to the man, I'm fully conversant with the history; I just don't think it's anything to be proud of!'

'My father's origins are in Ireland,' Madison mused thoughtfully. 'But we've never bothered to look them up.'

'And your mother?'

Madison turned to look out of the window. 'Also of Irish descent,' she murmured dismissively, reminded that she really must telephone her mother. Unless she wanted her mother to come looking for her! 'Oh, look at the seals in the bay!' She pointed excitedly as she saw the grey heads bobbing in the water in what had been signposted Port Erin Bay.

Claire nodded as she parked the car. 'We sometimes get basking sharks in here too.'

'And to think I had never heard of the Isle of Man until a month ago!' Madison murmured ruefully.

'We like to keep the beauty and tranquillity of the place to ourselves; if we told everyone how lovely it is here we would be inundated with visitors and people wanting to live here!' Claire said.

Madison certainly felt refreshed from their drive out. So much so that when they returned to the house she encouraged Claire in her idea of going out for the evening to see her parents, refusing the other woman's invitation for her to join her. Gideon wasn't back yet, and it would give her a few hours to herself to study the script in peace and quiet.

It was a little after eight, while she was sitting curled up on the sofa with her script, when she heard Gideon's key in the door, and some of her earlier tension returned at once. But she quickly dampened that down, determined to meet him as normally as possible. The tension that had been between them since last night would have to be ignored if they were to work together. If not forgotten…

'Hi.' She walked out to the kitchen to greet him, her hair loose about her shoulders, looking very slender in her green silk sweater and fitted denims, with her feet bare. 'I thought I heard a car.'

Gideon had his back towards her as he looked in the fridge, his shoulders tensing, before he too seemed to make a concerted effort to relax. He turned slowly to face her. 'I picked up another hire car in town; there's no way the three of us can manage with one car between us.'

But even with two cars, that still left Madison having to drive everywhere with either Gideon or Claire… She would have to see later in the week about getting herself a car of her own to drive.

'I thought with the car gone the two of you must have gone out to eat,' Gideon added huskily. 'I was looking to see if there was anything I could get myself for dinner.'

Madison looked at him closely, noting the tired shadows under his eyes. He had been hit over the head with a bottle on Saturday evening, spent most of yesterday in hospital, and the majority of today travelling and then working; he looked exhausted.

'Claire has gone out to see her parents,' she told him briskly. 'But I haven't eaten yet, either, and there are some eggs and salad in the fridge. Could make us both an omelette to go with the salad?' she offered tentatively, aware herself of just how domesticated the suggestion sounded—and Gideon was the least domesticated man she knew!

His brows rose, as if he too saw the irony of their situation, but he didn't voice his derision, merely nodded. 'You make the omelettes, I'll do the salad and make the dressing.'

To say she was relieved at the release from his sarcasm, for even a few minutes, was an understatement. Every time they'd spoken to each other today it had ended up in verbal warfare, and quite frankly she found it all a little tiresome—as well as nerve-racking!

The next fifteen minutes proved they could be relaxed in each other's company—or, at least, that they could *act* as if they were!—the two of them preparing the simple meal together in quiet harmony. Something that Madison hadn't thought would ever happen after last night—

Forget last night, she ordered herself firmly. Gideon certainly seemed to have done so since his return, and if he could do it so could she.

'This is good,' Gideon commented after his first mouthful of the fluffy omelette.

She grinned. 'Us starving actresses have to be able to make inexpensive food appetising,' she teased. Although she would be lying if she denied being pleased at his compliment...

Gideon tilted his head in thought as he looked at her. 'Somehow, Madison, you don't come over as a starving actress,' he finally drawled.

He was right, of course; her family was far too wealthy for her to ever have to starve in anything she chose to do. She'd always been aware that she had a privileged background. But, even so, she leant on her family for financial support as little as possible, determined to make it on her own.

'I wasn't being insulting, Madison.' Gideon sighed heavily at her lack of reply. 'Damn it, I seem to have lost the art of light, meaningless conversation!' he put down his knife and fork, scowling at his own inadequacy.

She smiled. 'I wasn't insulted, Gideon,' she assured him huskily. 'And, quite frankly, I doubt you ever had it. "The art of light, meaningless conversation!"' she explained at his impatient glance.

He gave a self-derisive grimace. 'You're probably right,' he acknowledged.

'And I think it's probably also a little late in the day for you to begin to learn it,' Madison teased.

'Eat your food, woman,' he growled with feigned impatience.

'That's better.' She nodded happily. 'Don't ever try and change, Gideon; no one would recognise you if you did!'

'You know, you're making me feel really good about myself!' he said with self-disgust. 'Am I really such an unreasonable tyrant?'

Madison opened her mouth to answer him, and then

thought better of it. After all, honesty wasn't always the best policy!

'I think I'll take the fifth on that, if you don't mind,' she finally answered, tongue-in-cheek.

Gideon chuckled. 'No one has ever spoken to me in quite the way you do.' He shook his head ruefully.

She quirked blonde brows at him. 'And?'

He shrugged. 'I wouldn't recognise you if you were to try and change, either,' he acknowledged huskily.

Somehow the conversation had taken a flirtatious turn, and for the moment Madison didn't want to call a halt to it...!

'Should I take that as a compliment?'

He looked at her steadily with those dark grey eyes. 'What do you think?' he finally returned softly.

'Oh, no,' she laughed, shaking her head. 'You tell me!'

They were passing the line of what was acceptable in their director/actress relationship. Madison's rapid pulse rate and shallow breathing told her that. But as this seemed to happen every time they were alone together she had no answer to how to stop it happening.

'The second one in as many minutes?' he murmured thoughtfully. 'I've already complimented you on your cooking,' he explained at her puzzled expression.

She nodded. 'Perhaps we had better just take it as a statement of fact.'

Gideon laughed softly. 'Perhaps we had. Would you like some white wine to go with your food?' He stood up as he made the offer, moving to the refrigerator. 'I bought some last week when I realised you and Claire would be here this week.'

She'd seen the bottles of wine in the fridge earlier, but, being aware of his aversion to alcohol, she hadn't even thought of getting one of them out to accompany their meal. And she wasn't sure it was a good idea for her to drink wine while Gideon remained completely sober…!

'A glass of wine would be lovely, thank you,' she heard herself accept smoothly.

It seemed her caution was being overridden by her love for this man!

Well…one glass couldn't do any harm, could it? she reasoned to herself. Who was she kidding? She instantly rebuked herself; Gideon was intoxicating enough on his own, without the added influence of wine! Well, it was too late to change her mind now. She would just stick to the one glass, and everything should be fine.

But it was rather a good bottle of Chablis, and as they ate and Madison drank she gave him an account of her drive around the island that afternoon.

'Great place, isn't it?' Gideon nodded enthusiastically. 'Full of atmosphere. And the best thing is that the film industry over here is still quite new, so film crews haven't become a nuisance to the islanders yet,' he added. 'Personally, I hope they never do; I think it's an excellent location.'

She nodded. 'Claire is obviously glad to be home for a couple of months.'

'You can take the woman out of the island, but you can't take the island out of the woman,' Gideon dryly misquoted. 'But she was a hundred per cent right about this place. If it wasn't for Claire suggesting I look at the Isle of Man, we would be in Ireland filming now,' he explained.

The two of them were chatting away like old friends, and considering the way they had parted the evening before, and the tension that had been between them this morning, that was quite refreshing in itself! Although Madison had no doubt that it wouldn't last; she was like the tinder to Gideon's flame!

In fact, she decided as she heard the sound of a car in the driveway, signalling Claire's return, the relaxed atmosphere between the two of them was probably about to end right now!

'I don't think Claire took the key,' Madison murmured as the front doorbell rang in the kitchen where the two of them sat.

'But she knows to come in the back door.' Gideon frowned in puzzlement as he slowly stood up.

Madison didn't move as he went out into the hallway to open the door, frowning as she sipped at her wine. If it was Claire at the front door, then the other woman was deliberately being discreet.

After the way Madison had become so upset over Gideon's behaviour earlier, perhaps that wasn't so surprising. Claire was far from being naive, and even though Madison had denied there was anything between herself and Gideon the other woman was sure to know that there was definitely some feeling on Madison's side towards Gideon. Why else had the other woman given that obscure warning about it being unwise to become emotionally involved with him?

But Gideon seemed to be a long time answering the door if it was only Claire, and after several minutes Madison got up to see what was keeping him.

She knew there was something seriously wrong even as she walked down the hallway; she could hear the soft murmur of voices, voices that were hushed with tension.

Gideon turned as he sensed Madison's presence behind him. 'Claire has been involved in an accident,' he told her bluntly, indicating the policeman who stood on the doorsteps. 'She's in hospital.'

Terrible images instantly flashed across her mind, and she looked at the policeman with apprehensive eyes.

'Cuts and bruises and a broken arm, Mrs Byrne,' he told her lightly. 'Nothing in the least life-threatening, I can assure you. In fact, I'm sorry to disturb you at this time of night, but Miss Christian's parents felt we should let the two of you know as she's actually staying here.'

Madison felt the hot colour enter her cheeks at being mistaken for Gideon's wife, looking to him to correct the other man. Which he didn't do!

'We'll go to the hospital straight away.' Gideon nodded tersely. 'Thank you for letting us know,' he added as the policeman turned to leave.

Madison quickly pushed aside the embarrassment of being mistaken for Gideon's wife, her mind racing. Poor Claire. It seemed that it never rained but it poured; first Gideon ended up in hospital, and now Claire. But what should she do about—?

'Move it, Madison,' Gideon instructed briskly, scowling darkly, their earlier ease with each other completely forgotten as he pushed past her to go and pick up his jacket.

Madison 'moved it', very worried about Claire herself. She would decide what to do next after she had seen and spoken to Claire...

What a hell of an end to what had been quite a pleasant evening!

Gideon hadn't been too sure of his reception from Madison after this morning, and had been pleasantly surprised when she appeared so warm and agreeable. He had enjoyed preparing the meal with her. And now this.

He'd grown very fond of Claire over the last five years, felt she was a friend rather than just an employee, and the two of them worked well together.

Besides, he wasn't sure it was a good idea for himself and Madison to be alone here at the house...

The two of them didn't talk on the drive to the hospital in Douglas. Gideon was worried about Claire, Madison also lost in her own thoughts. Although he couldn't help wondering what those thoughts might be...

But he could guess at what one of them might be! 'Don't give the policeman's remark another thought,' he told Madison dismissively as the two of them entered the hospital through the automatically opening doors.

She gave him a startled look. 'What?'

He sighed impatiently. 'I thought it was less embarrassing, for everyone, if I didn't correct him on his mistake over our marital status—or lack of it,' he bit out irritably. 'I'm sure men and women co-habiting is as normal on the island as it is anywhere else; I just didn't think it appropriate at the time to correct the man.' And he wished now he had never started this conversation!

Thank goodness they were almost at the ward where the policeman had told him Claire had been admitted! Why couldn't he have just left the subject alone? It wasn't important. It had just occurred to him that Madison herself could be getting worked up about it. Although why the hell should she?

But, of course, he was forgetting Simon Cauley! The last thing Madison would want—even though Gideon considered the possibility very remote—was for the other man to ever learn she had been passing herself off as Gideon's wife while the two of them stayed on the Isle of Man, especially as she'd only just renewed her acquaintance with Simon…!

Somehow that realisation made him feel incredibly angry!

'We can only stay a few minutes,' he told Madison harshly after speaking to the sister of the ward. 'Apparently Claire is sedated at the moment, so she won't be able to talk to us anyway.'

'Fine,' Madison accepted, seeming slightly dazed by the coldness of his tone.

Hell, he didn't seem to do anything right where this woman was concerned. But remembering her relationship with Simon Cauley wasn't conducive to improving his mood.

Claire looked awful! There was no other way to describe the 'cuts and bruises' the policeman had told them about. She looked as if she had gone straight through the windscreen, smashing the glass as she did so!

Madison gasped at his side, obviously as shocked as he was by Claire's condition, staring down at the other woman with tears hovering on the edges of her long, golden lashes.

Gideon had never been able to remain detached from a woman's tears. His mother had cried so much after his father had died, and Gideon had been the only one there to dry them from her cheeks.

He moved to dry Madison's tears too, taking a tissue from the box on the table beside Claire's bed. 'It looks worse than it actually is,' he assured her softly, hoping he was speaking the truth—because at the moment Claire didn't look very well at all.

Madison turned to bury her face in his shoulder. 'I didn't think—didn't expect— Oh, Gideon, poor Claire. And we were sitting at home enjoying our dinner, thinking she was having a lovely evening with her family!' Her slender shoulders shook as she cried in earnest. 'She'll be all right, won't she, Gideon?' Her eyes were drenched with tears as she looked up at him.

Gideon felt the breath catch in his throat. This woman got to him in a way no other woman ever had, touched something inside him he'd thought long dead. If it had ever been alive in him. He'd cared for his mother, had loved her, but there had been no other woman who'd even come close to touching that tender side of him. Until Madison, he realised, with an inward groan.

And he didn't want to feel those emotions towards Madison McGuire, either!

He put her abruptly away from him. 'She'll be fine,' he

dismissed harshly. 'And she won't want to see you blubbing all over her when she wakes up, so no more tears!' He deliberately didn't look at Madison again, although he could feel her outraged glance on him.

Good. An angry Madison he could deal with, but a tearful one he just couldn't cope with. Not until he got his own emotions, where Madison was concerned, under control.

If he ever did...

But not doing so was a possibility he wouldn't even allow for—couldn't allow for. He'd seen what loving someone did to a man. His own father had betrayed his family because he'd fallen in love with another woman, had drunk himself to death because of his love for that woman. Gideon would never allow that to happen to him. Never!

Love...?

Why the hell had that word come into his thoughts? He wasn't in love with Madison. He was attracted to her, wanted her, desired her, but that wasn't love!

'Let's get out of here,' he grated coldly. 'We can't do anything for Claire tonight, and we sure as hell aren't doing anything for you,' he added cruelly, his brows raised as he looked pointedly at her tear-stained face.

He was rewarded for that cruelty by seeing the colour fade from Madison's cheeks as she put a self-conscious hand up to her blotched face, swallowing hard before she turned away, bending to gently kiss Claire on a spot on her cheek that wasn't cut or bruised, before walking from the room, her back straight, her head held high.

Gideon had hurt her, deliberately so. But the alternative—of having her cry on his shoulder once again—would have been unbearable to him at the moment. He couldn't be responsible for his own reaction. Not that he would ever tell her that. No way!

He said his own goodnight to Claire, finding Madison waiting outside in the corridor for him, the two of them falling into step as they walked out of the hospital together. But they didn't talk, Gideon because he had nothing to say, and Madison, he presumed, because she was still angry with him.

He wanted to keep her that way!

'Drink?' he offered tersely once they were back at the house. 'Coffee or something?'

'No, thanks.' She stood just inside the doorway to the kitchen. 'If you don't mind, I think I'll just go straight to bed.'

'Why the hell should I mind?' He sat down at the kitchen table, picking up the glass of wine Madison had abandoned earlier, taking a sip from it before he realised what he was doing. Disgusted, he slammed the glass back down on the table as he turned to look at her accusingly. 'What are you staring at?' he challenged harshly.

She looked at the wine glass he had so recently sipped from, and then back at him, obviously having noticed the lapse. And she was drawing her own conclusions from it.

Well, let her.

Damn it, he wasn't answerable to Madison McGuire or any other woman for what he did or didn't do. He never had been. And he never would be!

CHAPTER TEN

MADISON was up early the next morning, but somehow she knew Gideon was up before her; she sensed he was awake somewhere in the house. And she could take a guess at the reason—he hadn't been able to sleep!

She was right. He was already in the kitchen drinking strong coffee made in the percolator when she came quietly into the room.

He glanced across at her before looking away again. 'Help yourself,' he said, pointing towards the coffee.

She poured herself a mug of the strong brew before sitting down opposite him at the kitchen table. Neither of them spoke, and as the minutes passed Madison could feel her tension rising.

Finally she could stand it no longer. 'Have you telephoned the hospital this morning?'

He nodded. 'Claire's awake. Which probably means she's in a lot of pain.' He scowled darkly. 'I'm going in to town to see her in a few minutes. Do you want to come?'

The invitation seemed grudging to Madison. And if what she had suspected last night were true, then she had a feeling Gideon would rather go in and see Claire on his own. Besides, she had somewhere else to go this morning.

She shook her head, unable to look up and meet his gaze. 'Give her my love, would you, and tell her I'll come in and see her later?'

He stood up abruptly. 'Sure,' he accepted tersely. 'When I get back I'll take you out to where we're shooting the film, introduce you to the rest of the crew. Okay?' he prompted hardly when she made no response.

'Okay,' she acknowledged dryly; hopefully she would either see him at the hospital or be back here herself before he returned.

But it was work as usual as far as Gideon was concerned, Madison thought incredulously after he had gone. The woman he loved was lying seriously ill in hospital, but the shooting of the film went on as planned. Because he did love Claire. That much had become obvious to her last night at the hospital.

He had been visibly shaken as the two of them stood in Claire's hospital room looking down at her pale face, with its numerous cuts. Possibly he had only just realised himself how he felt about her, which was why he had been unable to hide his feelings. Normally Gideon didn't like to give away any of his emotions!

Madison had been devastated by the realisation, had been stunned into silence herself. She had only recently discovered her own love for him, and he was in love with someone else. And, to make matters worse, it was with a woman she was proud to call her friend. It might have been much easier if she disliked the woman Gideon loved!

But if Gideon thought he was the only one who loved Claire, then he was in for a disappointment, Madison thought sadly as she telephoned for a taxi to take her to the airport.

The morning flight from Heathrow was on time. Edgar was one of the first to come through from the arrivals lounge, the overnight bag he carried meaning he probably hadn't had to collect any baggage and had just walked off the plane straight out to where Madison anxiously awaited him.

But Madison's anxiety turned to blank disbelief as she saw the two people who followed behind him. It couldn't be—! How on earth—? When—? How—?

Her mother and her brother...!

'I'll explain later,' Edgar rasped as he reached her and saw her totally stunned expression at the sight of her family. 'How is she?'

He looked every one of his sixty-two years at this moment, had obviously spent a sleepless night himself after Madison had telephoned him the previous evening to tell him of Claire's accident.

As soon as she'd seen Claire last night, Madison had known that she would have to call Edgar—because if she was right, Claire had been the woman in Edgar's bedroom when she'd come home unexpectedly on Sunday evening, so Edgar would want to know Claire had been injured in a car crash…

She'd waited until she heard Gideon go to bed the previous evening before creeping back downstairs again to use the telephone, all the time on edge in case Gideon should hear her. She'd known from Edgar's distressed reaction to the news, that her suspicion about a relationship between him and Claire had been correct.

There had been something slightly unnatural about the way Claire had been sitting in the kitchen drinking coffee with Edgar yesterday morning when Madison had got up. Although the two of them had talked as if Claire had only just arrived, somehow it hadn't rung true to Madison. And then, of course, there had been Claire's hot date the previous evening…

Edgar's response to her call had been instant. He'd said he would book himself on the morning flight to the island, would be here by nine-thirty. He just hadn't mentioned anything about bringing her mother and Jonny with him!

But none of that was important at this moment. Edgar was obviously anxious to hear about Claire. 'Gideon telephoned the hospital earlier, and Claire is awake. He's at the hospital with her now,' she added reluctantly.

The two men didn't seem to get on at the best of times,

but when they both learnt they were in love with the same woman…!

She turned to her mother and brother, giving them both a hug, although she had to force the welcoming smile to her lips. It wasn't that she wasn't pleased to see them, she just wondered what on earth they were doing here. Edgar hadn't mentioned they were in England, let alone that he would be bringing them to the island with him this morning!

'Madison—'

'Not now, Susan,' Edgar cut in as her mother would have spoken to her. 'You can sort out your problems with Madison at some other time. At the moment I'm only interested in seeing with my own eyes that Claire is okay,' he added grimly, turning towards the exit, and obviously expecting them all to follow him.

'Gideon…?' her mother bit out sharply as she fell into step beside Madison, Jonny bringing up the rear as they emerged into the late spring sunshine.

'I said not now, Susan,' Edgar turned to growl aggressively, using a tone of voice with her mother that Madison, for one, had never heard him use to her before. 'You chose to come here; no one invited you. If the circumstances aren't to your liking, that's just too damned bad!'

She put her hand sympathetically on her mother's arm as she saw her wince at the attack. 'He's very worried at the moment.' She excused his uncharacteristic harshness.

Her mother nodded. 'Claire seems—very important to him.'

But she was also important to Gideon. And somehow Madison didn't think Gideon was going to thank her for contacting the older man, let alone having met him at the airport and brought him to the hospital!

But she couldn't help that. It was Claire she was thinking of. And, no matter what Gideon might have realised about his own feelings towards a woman he had only previously thought of as his assistant, it was Edgar that Claire was involved with. In those circumstances, it was Edgar the other woman would want to see…

Edgar sat in the front of the taxi beside the driver, the other three squeezed in the back together, Madison seated next to her brother.

'What are you doing here?' she prompted him in a fierce whisper. Jonny ran the family business with their father, and it must have been something important that had dragged him away from doing that.

He shrugged his broad shoulders, looking distinctly uncomfortable with his athletically fit bulk squashed between the two women. 'I have no idea,' he drawled dryly. 'Mom grew tired of Edgar putting her off with excuses as to why you couldn't talk to her on the telephone and decided she was coming to England to see for herself what was going on.' He shrugged again. 'Dad couldn't get away just now, but you know him—he wasn't prepared to let Mom travel on her own, either. I was nominated to come with her.' And he didn't sound particularly happy about it, either.

She should have made a point of telephoning her mother. Madison inwardly rebuked herself. Then this meeting need never have happened. There just hadn't been the time since Edgar had told her of her mother's call on Sunday night…

Oh, well, there was nothing she could do about it now. She would take Edgar to the hospital, show him to Claire's room, and then she could deal with her mother and Jonny.

But as she chanced a brief look at her mother, around her brother's body, the look on her face wasn't encouraging!

Oh, for goodness' sake; she was twenty-two years old, not a baby any more, and at some stage her mother was going to have to realise that. It looked as if that time had come!

Madison swallowed hard. Somehow she knew Gideon, with his desire that she keep a very low profile, was not going to be pleased at the arrival on the island of most of her family—one member of it in particular!

She hadn't even started work on the movie yet, and after today she perhaps never would, once Gideon had met her mother. Because then he would realise his chances of keeping Madison low-profile for any length of time would probably be nil!

'We'll come in with you,' her mother decided as the taxi drew to a halt outside the hospital. She climbed gracefully out of the car on to the pavement, Jonny dutifully following her.

Madison frowned across at her mother. Her idea had been to take Edgar in herself, and then come back and rejoin her family. Edgar and Gideon could then fight it out between them as to who had the most right to be at Claire's side. But one look at the determination in her mother's green eyes, the stubborn set of her mouth, and Madison knew she might as well save her breath in even making that suggestion.

So much for any desire to delay a confrontation with Gideon; he would take one look at her mother and want to know exactly what the hell was going on! Especially when he realised she *was* Madison's mother. Because her mother—tiny, blonde, elegant, and still extremely beautiful in her mid-fifties—was instantly recognisable as the movie star Susan Delaney...!

Gideon believed he had found himself an unknown for his movie, and had chosen Madison as his star for that very reason. But her mother was anything but that, and she didn't think Gideon was going to be too happy about it. She had hoped that Gideon wouldn't need to know about her mother until after they had made the movie, when it wouldn't really matter any more, because—she hoped!—

her own talent would have proved enough for him not to
give a damn who her mother was. Fate, it seemed—in the
guise of her mother's unexpected arrival now—had decided
otherwise.

She only hoped Gideon wasn't going to be too annoyed,
either with her or with Edgar. Because it was going to be
obvious to Gideon that the older man, being Madison's
godfather, had known of her mother's celebrity status from
the outset.

Annoyed didn't quite describe the look on Gideon's face
when he turned and saw Edgar enter Claire's hospital room
at Madison's side; he looked absolutely furious!

He stood up with a scraping of the chair he had been
sitting on next to Claire's bed. 'What the hell are you doing—?' He broke off, having looked past them to the other
couple who had entered the room.

Annoyed didn't describe the look on his face as he
looked at Madison's mother and brother, either! He gave
the latter only a cursory glance, but her mother—!

His eyes had narrowed to steely slits, his face rigid, a
grey tinge to his skin as he continued to stare at Madison's
mother. 'You!' he finally spat out harshly. 'What—?'

'It's all right, Gideon.' Madison rushed forward to put
her hand on his arm, hoping to stop him before he could
do or say anything unforgivable. She'd known he wasn't
going to be pleased at finding out her mother was a famous
actress in her own right, but the whole situation would become completely impossible if, in his anger at feeling he
had been duped, he also became insulting. 'You see—'

'No, it is *not* all right, damn you!' he shook her hand off
roughly, all of his attention still centred on Madison's
mother. 'What are you doing here?' he bit out icily.

Her mother drew herself up to her full height of five feet
two inches. 'Gideon—'

'Don't call me that,' he cut in harshly. 'Don't ever call

me that! In fact, I would prefer it if you didn't speak to me at all!' He turned furiously to Edgar. 'What the hell are you playing at, Remington? What is *she* doing here?' His hands were clenched into fists at his sides.

Madison was dazed by Gideon's absolute fury at seeing her mother. She'd known he wouldn't be too happy once he knew who her mother was, but his reaction seemed out of all proportion with the little deceit she had practised. She had figured that with his desire for an unknown, if he knew she was the daughter of a famous actress he wouldn't give her the part. Now she wished she'd been more honest...

'Behave yourself, Gideon!' Edgar turned briefly from where he stood at the bedside holding Claire's hand, the tension having disappeared from his face now that he had assured himself that Claire, although obviously injured, wouldn't suffer any lasting damage from the accident.

'Behave myself?' Gideon repeated in controlled fury. 'You bring *that* woman here—and you expect me to remain calm? You—'

'I have no idea who you might be—' Jonny stepped forward, his voice soft, but edged with warning '—but I would advise you not to talk to, or about, my mother in that contemptuous tone again!' He met the other man's gaze with icy challenge.

Gideon looked at him with disdainful scorn. 'And who the hell might you be—besides her son, of course?'

'I warned you not to talk about my mother in that way—'

'Jonny!' Madison cried as she stepped forward, putting her hand on her brother's arm just as he would have struck the other man; this whole thing was spiralling out of control!

Something was so wrong, so very wrong...!

Gideon turned to include her in his anger now. 'Jonny?'

he repeated disgustedly. 'Are you telling me that your boy-friend Jonny is *that* woman's son?'

'Damn it, I warned you…!'

Before Madison was aware of what was happening, Jonny's arm had swung out and he had hit the other man, Gideon staggering backwards from the blow, although he didn't fall; he quickly regained his balance, before swinging his own arm back and aiming a blow towards Jonny's chin.

'What on earth is going on here?'

An astonished nurse stood in the doorway, obviously well aware that there was a fight taking place in the room of one of her patients—and horrified at the fact!

With just cause, Madison conceded dazedly. Her brother and Gideon had just *hit each other*!

'I think you should all leave,' the nurse told them stiffly.

'But—'

The scowl the nurse gave Edgar instantly silenced him. 'Miss Christian was involved in an accident last night. She's still in need of rest and quiet. Visiting time is later this afternoon, when you may visit two at a time,' she added, pointedly holding the door open for them to leave.

Which they all did, slowly. Jonny was nursing his punched jaw, his mother's usual calm replaced by obvious distress, Gideon glaring at them both as they preceded him. Madison gave Edgar a slightly dazed look before she also left the room. Edgar remained only a few seconds longer so that he could make his goodbye in private to Claire before joining them.

'Well, I hope you're proud of yourself,' he snapped at Gideon once they were outside on the pavement.

'*I'm* proud of myself?' Gideon repeated icily, his fury unmistakable. 'Don't even try to lay the blame for this on me, Edgar! You must have known all the time that Madison is involved with this Jonny character, which must also mean you've also known exactly who his mother is. You—'

'I'm afraid that isn't quite right, Gideon,' Madison was the one to put in quietly. It was time someone put a halt to all this misunderstanding.

And minutes ago she'd realised something that meant it had to be sooner rather than later!

She'd always thought Gideon reminded her of someone, but until today, until a few minutes ago, she hadn't realised who that someone was. But as she'd looked around the hospital room at all the furious faces she had suddenly known exactly who Gideon reminded her of.

What she didn't know was *why*.

But before the day was out she was determined that she would know the answer to that, too…!

Gideon turned to look at Madison, so angry he couldn't think straight. And the reason for that was standing only feet away from him. Susan Delaney!

He'd hated her for most of his life, and now, completely without warning, she had just strolled back into his life. That she knew who he was too he didn't doubt; that one simple murmuring of his name had told him that much!

And Madison was involved with her son!

'In what way isn't it right?' he prompted scornfully. 'He's *her* son, *you're* involved with him—'

'No, Jonny!' Madison stepped forward, her hand once again on his arm as she restrained him from going into physical defence of his mother.

Gideon wished she would stop touching the other man in that way; it made him feel as murderously angry as coming face to face with Susan Delaney had done a few minutes ago!

Madison turned back to him. 'You're under a misapprehension concerning my relationship to Jonny,' she told him quietly. 'You see—'

'Madison, I don't believe a public sidewalk is the correct place to have this conversation,' Susan Delaney put in quietly after several people had walked by and given them curious looks for the obvious heated exchange that was taking place, shooting Gideon a quelling glance as he would have cut in on her remark.

She was still beautiful, he would give her that, Gideon acknowledged grudgingly. Thirty years ago she had been stunning, with beautiful golden hair, a breathtakingly lovely face and an hourglass figure, and maturity had only given more character to her face, and a mature allure to her figure.

Yes, she was more beautiful than ever, but Gideon knew, better than most, how that beauty hid a treacherous heart.

'No place would be the right place for this conversation,' he told Susan Delaney scornfully. 'And, quite frankly, I have no wish to hear anything *you* might have to say,' he added insultingly. 'Control that short fuse, buddy,' Gideon advised Jonny harshly as he again tensed in his mother's defence. 'Maybe it's you your mother should be talking to; you obviously don't have a clue just what a bit—'

'That's enough, Gideon.' Edgar briskly took charge of the situation. 'We are going to get into a couple of taxis—'

'I have my own transport, thank you,' Gideon assured him with arrogant dismissal.

'Okay, a taxi—and a car,' Edgar amended with a warning glance in his direction. 'Then we're going back to the house where you're all staying. And we're going to sit down and talk about this like the grown-up people we all are,' he added pointedly.

They might all be grown-up, but there was no way Gideon was going to sit down and talk to Susan Delaney about anything. Unless it was to ask her how many other lives she had wrecked during the last thirty years!

And as for Madison, he was no longer sure how to even look at her, let alone anything else, now that he knew she was involved with the Delaney family!

She stood slightly apart from all of them now, her green eyes swimming with unshed tears, a look of total bewilderment on her face.

She looked so young, damn it, so vulnerable, that part of him wanted to go to her and put his arms about her, to reassure her that everything was going to be okay. But he would be lying if he did that. Because unless she could assure him she would have nothing more to do with the Delaney family it would never be okay between them again…!

'I don't think so, thank you, Edgar,' he began dismissively. 'I—'

'It wasn't a request, Gideon,' the older man cut in harshly. 'It's time—way past time!—that all this was sorted out once and for all.'

'It's sorted, Edgar,' he assured the other man hardly. 'I want these two—' he indicated Susan Delaney and her son '—off the island on the first available plane—'

'You can't do that, Gideon,' Madison gasped in shocked dismay.

'No, he damn well can't,' Jonny put in contemptuously. 'As far as I'm aware, you don't own the damned island, Mr—Mr—'

'Byrne,' Edgar put in softly. 'His name is Gideon Byrne, Jonny.'

It was as if Edgar had struck the younger man, his recoil on hearing Gideon's name completely spontaneous, his gaze wary now as he looked at Gideon with narrowed eyes.

So, Jonny had heard of him, Gideon realised scornfully. His mother had confessed all her sins, then, he thought scathingly. Not quite what he would have expected from what he knew of her, but then that was her business. As he'd already said, he wasn't interested in anything she had to say.

He turned to Madison, his gaze steely. 'It seems your boyfriend and his mother intend staying for a while. If that's the case, I don't want either of them anywhere near the house, or near my film. In fact—'

She drew in a ragged breath, shaking her head. 'Gideon—'

'I think we've all been made aware of what you do and don't want, Gideon,' Edgar interrupted harshly. 'But I can assure you that it is in your best interest to come back to the house with us now and hear what needs to be said.'

Gideon turned angrily to face the older man, his gaze narrowing as he saw how determined Edgar looked. But in actual fact none of this had anything to do with Edgar. He wasn't even sure what the other man was doing here!

Except he had seemed, on reflection, very close to Claire earlier at the hospital… In fact, Gideon believed he had seen Edgar holding Claire's hand at one stage!

What the hell was going on here?

He shook his head. He could sort that out with Claire at some other time. What was important now was that he get away from Susan Delaney—and all the memories she'd brought with her!

'There's nothing that needs to be said—'

'I'm afraid there is, Gideon,' Madison cut in quietly, moving to lightly touch his arm.

Gideon looked down at her, frowning as he saw the pained look on her beautiful face. Damn it, he hadn't meant to hurt or upset her, knew she was the innocent one in all of this; it was just unfortunate that her involvement with Jonny had brought Susan back into his life…!

'It's nothing I want to hear, Madison,' he told her gruffly, briefly covering her hand with his own. 'I'll explain it all to you some other time. Or your boyfriend can!' he added hardly, shooting Jonny a look of intense dislike.

And it wasn't just because he was Susan Delaney's son! This man, tall, dark, and good-looking, was involved with Madison—and that made Gideon almost as angry as discovering whose son he was!

Madison gave a negative movement of her head. 'Jonny doesn't need to explain anything to me,' she murmured huskily, shooting her mother a pained grimace. 'Nothing at all,' she added softly.

Gideon moved sharply away from Madison's hand resting on his arm, his gaze cold now as he looked down at her. 'Then you knew from the beginning of the connection between—'

'No!' she cut in brokenly. 'No, I didn't realise that until a short time ago. But—'

'I don't believe you.' Gideon raked his gaze scathingly over all of them. 'You—'

'She didn't know of any connection, Gideon,' Susan Delaney was the one to murmur huskily, her gaze unflinching as he looked at her coldly. 'In fact, she still doesn't know,' she added gently, looking at Madison with beseeching eyes. 'Not everything.' She shook her head sadly, before once again looking at Gideon, her chin raised defensively. 'And neither do you,' she told him firmly. 'You were a child, Gideon, only seven years of age—'

His eyes blazed furiously. 'Old enough to know you stole my father from my mother—'

'People can't be stolen, Gideon,' she reproved softly.

'Okay, tempted, then,' he amended scornfully, his mouth twisting contemptuously. 'Whichever way you look at it, my father left my mother because he fell in love with you. Can you deny that?' he spat out distastefully.

She swallowed hard. 'No. But—'

'Of course you can't,' Gideon bit out derisively. 'You—'

'Gideon, this is not the place for this!' Edgar thundered furiously, moving protectively towards Susan Delaney as she swayed on her feet, his arm about her waist now as he held her tightly against his side.

'Not you too, Edgar!' Gideon realised with a disgusted shake of his head. 'Every man she meets seems to fall in love with her! The woman is—'

'My mother, Gideon,' Madison put in quietly.

'—nothing but—' He broke off abruptly, staring disbelievingly at Madison as her words slowly penetrated the angry fog in his brain. Had she just said—?

'Susan Delaney is my mother, Gideon,' she repeated softly. 'And Jonny is my brother,' she added as if to clarify the point, glancing uncertainly at the woman who was her mother, before looking back at Gideon, her chin raised defensively.

As Susan Delaney's had been seconds ago—as *Madison's mother's* had been seconds ago!

God, he had known from the beginning that Madison reminded him of someone; that golden hair, the shape of her face—hell, their eyes were even that same emerald-green!—but that the similarity was to Susan Delaney, because she was Madison's *mother*, had never even entered his head.

Although he did recall thinking he'd found himself dwelling more on the past—his mother's unhappiness, his father's death, his own disrupted childhood—since that first meeting with Madison…

It was the name that had thrown him, of course; there was no possibility there could ever have been a connection made by him between the two surnames McGuire and Delaney.

Deliberately so?

But if so, by whom?

Edgar had known. He had to have known. Because he

had known Gideon's father, and Susan Delaney, all those years ago. He was also Madison's godfather. He also had to be fully aware that, as Susan Delaney's daughter, Madison was the very last woman he would ever want to meet, let alone have star in one of his films. And Edgar had said nothing. Damn it, he had initiated the meeting between Madison and Gideon!

And Madison—what about Madison? Had she been in on the deception from the first? Madison said not. Her mother said the same thing—but then, Susan Delaney was the last woman he had reason ever to believe about anything!

His mouth twisted as he now included Madison in that look of intense dislike, although for the moment his attention was centred on her brother. 'You're right, Delaney— or is it McGuire...?' He seemed to remember there was a father somewhere called Malcolm McGuire...?

'McGuire,' the man Jonny confirmed hardly.

He gave an acknowledging inclination of his head. 'I don't own this island—but I do own the film rights to *Rosemary*,' he added harshly. 'I also have complete yea or nay over who is cast in my film—'

'Madison has a contract, Gideon,' Edgar put in quietly. 'And so, incidentally, do you.'

'I haven't finished yet, Edgar,' he told the other man with icy calm. 'And I would advise you not to threaten me,' he warned softly. 'I don't respond well to threats.'

Edgar glacially returned is unwavering gaze. 'You'll find neither do I!'

Gideon gave a humourless smile. 'I already know where you stand in all this, Edgar—and it isn't favourably, I can assure you!' He turned back to Madison. 'I'm also in a position to choose who I share a house with, and so I think the best thing you can do is clear your stuff out before I get back there. Otherwise you'll find it—and you—put outside on the doorstep!' He ignored her pained gasp at his deliberate cruelty, turning on his heel and walking away.

And he kept on walking until he reached the car, didn't falter a step. But it was his pride that kept him so rigid in his mobility. Because at this moment it was the only thing that stopped him from falling apart.

Madison…!

He might have ignored her pain just now, but that didn't mean he was immune to it. Far from it. She had looked so hurt, so bewildered, so incredibly *beautiful*!

But she was the one woman in all the world that he simply dared not allow himself to—

No!

He would get over this. Would get over Madison.

He would have to—because he could never let Susan Delaney's daughter into his life.

Not now. Or at any time in the future…!

CHAPTER ELEVEN

MADISON looked numbly across at her mother, the four of them, Edgar and Jonny included, back in the sitting-room of the house Gideon had rented. Madison hadn't known where else to take them, and by tacit consent they hadn't spoken about any of the scene that had taken place at the hospital until now, when Madison was sure they wouldn't be interrupted. From what Gideon had said to her before he left, he wouldn't be returning for some time.

Not until he was sure enough time had passed for her to have moved her things, and herself, out!

She drew in a shaky breath. 'Gideon doesn't know, does he?' she said dully. How could Gideon know? She hadn't realised the truth herself until a short time ago! And she'd been so stunned by the enormity of her discovery that Gideon's reaction at the identity of her mother as Susan Delaney had faded into the background.

'Madison!' Her mother gave a pained groan, sitting forward in her seat, her hands held out imploringly. 'It isn't what you think. It isn't what Gideon thinks, either,' she added, shaking her head. 'I was never involved in an affair with his father—'

'That's the truth, Madison,' Edgar put in grimly as she made a protesting sound. 'I knew Susan, and John Byrne, all those years ago, and Gideon's version of what happened isn't the correct one.'

'*He* believes it is,' Madison pointed out.

'I'm aware of that.' Edgar nodded abruptly. 'Which is why I thought it was time the record was put straight.'

'*You* thought?' Madison's mother looked at him disbelievingly. 'I realise now that you must have instigated all of this, but, Edgar, you had no right—'

'You've seen Gideon now, Susan,' Edgar cut in gently, going to stand beside her chair, looking down at her with gentle compassion. 'He was a young boy when all of that happened—and now he's a man, who cares for no one and allows no one to care for him, either,' he added in a pained voice.

Madison knew all too well how true that was—but she had fallen in love with him anyway. And it was a love that, even if Gideon had been a man who could ever fall in love with anyone, would never be returned; she was the last person Gideon would ever be able to love! And he didn't know the whole truth yet... How much greater his anger was going to be when he did know!

'You could have talked to me about it first, Edgar,' her mother reproved huskily, her face pale. 'But instead of that I opened a newspaper on Sunday morning and saw a photograph of Gideon Byrne at a film première—with my daughter hanging on to his arm!' She swallowed hard at the shock she had received on seeing the publication. 'His "mystery friend" was no mystery to me!'

Madison turned to look at her brother. 'Simon sends his regards,' she told him quietly.

Jonny nodded before turning back to their mother. 'Mom, this has been as much, if not more, of a shock to Madison as it has to you.' He gave Madison a rueful look. 'You love the guy, don't you...?' he prompted gently.

She swallowed. Yes, she loved the guy—for all the good it would do her!

Jonny didn't need an answer to his question, the distress on her face enough; he looked across at Edgar with flinty eyes. 'Did you take that into account when you did your thinking, Edgar?' he rasped angrily. 'Did you really stop to think what a Pandora's box you were opening by introducing Madison to Gideon?'

Edgar drew in a sharp breath. 'As a matter of fact, I did,' he answered hardly. 'Gideon has been completely alone in the world since his mother died ten years ago. He was bitter enough before then, but in the years since he's become so hard and cynical it's almost impossible to reach him. It's all right for you, Jonny,' he continued firmly as Madison's brother would have interrupted. 'You have people who love you—a family,' he added pointedly.

'That still didn't give you the right to interfere like this, Edgar,' Madison's mother said agitatedly. 'As Jonny had just said, you've opened up a part of our lives that was better left as a closed book.'

'Better for whom?' Edgar challenged impatiently. 'I've watched Gideon grow up, seen what the past has done to him. And although this touches you—obviously—I no longer think it was just your decision to make. Maybe I should have discussed it with you, but I— Gideon has no one, Susan. He's grown up believing his father left not only his mother, but him as well, because he loved someone else—you!—more than he loved either of them. Do you have any idea what effect that has had on him over the years? Of course you don't.' He shook his head. 'I've never had children of my own, and Gideon is about as close as I've ever come to having a son. I made a decision, rightly or wrongly, that it was time he knew he isn't alone in the world, after all.' He looked challengingly at Madison's mother and brother.

Madison looked at them, too. She had seen Jonny's reaction when told of Gideon's identity, knew in that moment that he was aware of exactly who the other man was.

'It's all right; I know Gideon is—' She broke off abruptly as the man in question strode arrogantly into the room, none of them having heard the arrival of his car as they'd sat talking so emotionally.

Madison paled when she saw the look of utter contempt on his face as he slowly looked around the room at them all, that hard gaze finally coming to rest on her.

'We weren't expecting you back just yet,' she murmured huskily; she hadn't ever expected to see him again!

'Obviously,' he scorned harshly. 'But as I have more right to be here than any of you I think I'll just sit here and wait for you all to leave.' He made himself comfortable in an armchair. 'Don't let me interrupt your conversation. You had got as far as "Gideon is"…?' he reminded her coldly.

As if she needed any reminding! She looked across at her mother, not knowing what she should do now. She couldn't just baldly come out with her original statement now—could she…?

Her mother's hands shook as she clasped them tightly together, her face paler still beneath her make-up. She inclined her head slightly.

Her mother wanted her to tell Gideon the truth! But what would that do to him? What was it going to do to all of them…?

She drew in a shaky breath, knowing that to delay wouldn't change anything, that this had gone too far now for Gideon not to be made aware of the truth. All of it. 'I was about to say,' she began shakily, 'to say—'

'No, Madison,' her mother cut in breathlessly. 'I'm not being fair to expect you to do this. I—' She stood up agitatedly, looking at Gideon. 'There's a lot you don't know about thirty years ago—'

'I know what I need to know,' he assured her scathingly.

'No, you don't.' She shook her head, suddenly looking every one of her fifty-three years.

Madison ached for her! She didn't need to know the whole truth about the past to know that she loved her mother, that nothing that would be said today, or at any other time, would, or ever could, change that love.

'No matter what else happened thirty years ago, there is one fact, one unchangeable fact, that—' Madison's mother faltered, her eyes swimming with unshed tears. 'That—'

'The truth is, Gideon,' Jonny was the one to take over the conversation, his hand on their mother's arm in gentle support '—that you're my brother!'

Madison gasped at the starkness of the statement. She had known it, guessed it—of course she had—but to actually hear the words...!

She had known it as she'd looked at the two men together in Claire's hospital room, had seen the similarity between the two men: the same dark hair, flinty grey eyes, the square jaw—even their height and build were the same.

Several times she'd felt that Gideon reminded her of someone—but there was no way, until she'd actually seen the two of them together, that she could ever have dreamt it was her own brother Gideon resembled!

Jonny had to be John Byrne's son and not, as Madison had always believed, the son of her own father, Malcolm McGuire...

Madison had no idea how that could be, especially when their mother denied ever having an affair with the legendary actor; she just knew it was a fact...

She looked at Gideon now, trying to gauge his reaction. There didn't seem to be one. He still sat in the armchair, his expression as contemptuous. Almost as if the statement had never been made...

Except that his eyes had taken on a silver sheen. And there was a nerve pulsing in his rigidly clenched jaw. But other than those two things he might just as well have been informed that it was quite mild for this time of year! Madison knew that she would have been knocked off her feet it someone had just told her that she had a brother she had never known existed. Although she supposed, as Gideon was already sitting down, that he couldn't be knocked off his feet!

But even as she watched him so apprehensively, waiting for some other outward sign that he was disturbed by what he had just heard, he turned easily to Edgar, giving the older man a derisive smile. 'I went back in to see Claire after you had all left,' he drawled. 'It seems the two of you have become more than a little—friendly, recently? To such an extent,' he added caustically, 'that the two of you were able to collude over the casting of Madison as Rosemary in my film!'

There was a ruddy hue in Edgar's cheeks now. 'I think ''collude'' is rather a strong word to use—'

'Do you?' Gideon cut in viciously. 'I think it more than adequately described Claire telling you which restaurants we were going to, Claire's championing of Madison, of her telephoning you when I ended up in hospital so that you could tell Madison.' He shook his head disgustedly. 'Any number of little incidents that didn't quite add up at the time, but which make perfect sense to me now!'

Madison had no idea where this conversation had even come from! Okay, so she'd worked out a lot of what he had just said for herself—but was Gideon going to say nothing about just being told he was Jonny's brother?

Edgar sighed heavily. 'I don't suppose there's any point in trying to explain to you exactly why we did those things?'

'None at all,' Gideon grated.

'And what Jonathan just told you?' Edgar prompted impatiently. 'I take it you did hear what he said—'

'Of course I heard what he said, damn you!' Gideon was on his feet now, that relaxed pose completely gone as he stood tensely in the middle of the room, his hands clenched at his sides, his expression savage.

'Gideon—'

'Don't, Madison!' he warned icily as she would have reached out to him, his eyes glittering dangerously as his gaze moved across each person in the room in turn. 'I heard the comment, Edgar,' he told the other man harshly. 'I simply chose to ignore it. I still choose to ignore it. And them.' He looked contemptuously at Madison's mother and brother.

Madison looked from her mother's palely distressed face and Jonny's set one to Gideon's stonily unyielding features. 'Look at Jonny, Gideon,' she pleaded brokenly. 'Please— just look at him!' she encouraged emotionally. 'Look at the likeness between the two of you! My father is blond and fair-skinned.' She'd never thought about that before, but now she realised it as a fact. Her mother was blonde too. 'Jonny is my brother, Gideon; I've never doubted that. But now I can see all too clearly that he's your brother too! Look at him, Gideon,' she pleaded again, tears streaming hotly down her cheeks now as her emotions became too much for her to even attempt to control. 'Just look at him…!'

He didn't want to look at Jonathan McGuire, the man they were all claiming—including Jonathan himself!—was his brother.

He'd been alone for so long—most of his life, it seemed, more of a support for his mother than she was parent to him after she and his father had separated. And he didn't want Jonathan McGuire, of all people, to be connected to him in any way. Certainly not as a brother!

He gave Susan Delaney a chilling look. 'You told me there was no affair,' he reminded her accusingly.

She chewed on her top lip, a habit he'd noticed with Madison when she was nervous or upset about something. But he had found the vulnerability provocative when

Madison did it; in his mind Susan Delaney was about as vulnerable as a piranha!

'There wasn't,' she finally murmured softly, before turning to Edgar with pleading eyes. 'Edgar, you started this— and now I have no idea how to tell Gideon what happened between his father and myself!'

'Don't even bother,' Gideon dismissed heavily, turning to Jonny with emotionless eyes. 'Even if what you said was true—'

'Oh, it's true, all right,' Jonny assured him grimly. 'My mother explained it all to me when I was eighteen. She talked it over with—my stepfather, Malcolm, and the two of them felt I should know who my real father was. John Byrne,' he added softly.

Gideon felt a physical pain in his chest. When he was a child he had loved his father with an emotion that bordered on adoration. He'd believed his father could capture the moon for him if he asked for it, and when his father had left his mother it had felt as if he had rejected Gideon too, that somehow he must have done something so that his father no longer wanted to be with him, either. Oh, he had still seen his father on what was called 'reasonable access', but more often than not his mother would become hysterical when the time came and the visit with his father would never happen.

And then his father had died, the suddenness of that death meaning there had been no chance to say goodbye to him, just a separation that had been final. But still unfinished, he recognised.

'Gideon,' Jonny said softly, 'would you take a walk outside with me?'

No! He didn't want to hear—

Come on, Gideon, you aren't seven years old any more, he inwardly rebuked himself. And, of course, he'd realised as he'd matured that what had happened between his parents, their separation and divorce, had happened to thousands of other couples too, thousands of other children; that a parent wasn't rejecting the child by leaving their partner, only acknowledging that they no longer loved the person they were married to.

He'd realised that—but the painful loss of his father had lingered, had coloured all of his own life, it seemed. And, ridiculous as it seemed, he didn't even want to share the memory of his father with a man who claimed John Byrne was his father too…!

He assumed an uninterested air. 'Sure.' He agreed to Jonny's suggestion. 'But nothing you have to say will make any difference to how I feel about this situation,' he added in warning as he turned to follow the other man from the room.

Jonny gave a rueful inclination of his head. 'That's your perogative.'

Gideon found Madison looking at him with tear-wet eyes as he drew level with her, the tears she hadn't been able to stop from overflowing earlier still dampening her cheeks. And for a brief moment Gideon was tempted to reach out and wipe away those tears, to caress her creamy cheeks, to reassure her that everything was going to be all right. Except that it wasn't.

He had been telling the truth earlier when he'd said he had gone back in to see Claire once they had all left in the taxi, but he had stayed with her only briefly, needing time to do some thinking of his own. And the conclusion of those thoughts made it impossible for him to even touch Madison. He simply didn't dare.

So instead of touching her he gave her a tight, meaningless smile before following Jonny outside.

The sun, it seemed, knew nothing of the darkness of their situation, and was shining brightly; birds were singing— gulls crying as they flew overhead in the light breeze.

The two men walked some way from the house in silence, to stand on the cliff that overlooked the gentle swell of the Irish Sea. They stood there for some time, neither inclined to break the peace of the silence that surrounded them.

Gideon didn't break that silence, but he did take the opportunity to do what Madison had pleaded with him to do earlier; he looked at Jonathan McGuire. Really looked at him.

He saw a tall man of about thirty, his build athletically fit, rugged rather than handsome, with dark hair that was inclined to curl, and metallic-grey eyes. Gideon saw himself as he had been a few years earlier...!

As if aware of his critical gaze, Jonny turned to look at him, giving a slight, humourless smile. 'Weird, isn't it?' he murmured softly, giving a slight shake of his head. 'Until Edgar told me earlier who you were, it hadn't even occurred to me...! But once I knew you were Gideon Byrne I—' He frowned. 'I know this probably sounds strange to you, but—seeing you is like finding the missing piece of a jigsaw puzzle!'

It didn't sound strange at all; in the last few minutes Gideon had realised he felt the same way. He had a brother! The how or why of it—well, that was too painful still to guess!—but that didn't change the fact that this man was his brother, that the same blood flowed through their veins: their father's blood.

But Jonathan was Madison's brother, too—Jonny, as she called him. God, how he had hated the man Jonny that she talked about, believing he was someone she was romantically involved with back home. But the fact that Jonny was her brother only made things more complicated—because he was Gideon's brother too. Hell, it might even make him and Madison related in some way...

'I still remember how I felt when my mother told me the

truth of my parentage when I was eighteen,' Jonny continued softly, once again gazing out to sea, his hands thrust into his trouser pockets. 'And don't take this wrong, Gideon, but the truth of the matter is I felt very little—had no interest in searching out this other family I seemed to have acquired. Malcolm had been my father from the day I was born, had always treated me as his real son. And none of what I was told that day made any difference to that. I still work with my father in the family business, and I probably always will. It was only today, when I saw the impact my existence as your brother had on you, that I realised that, without my even being aware of it, something had been missing from my life.' He frowned.

Gideon's mouth twisted. 'The missing link, hmm?' he murmured self-derisively. 'Is this the point in the conversation where we're supposed to fall into each other's arms like—?'

'Long-lost brothers?' Jonny quirked dark brows humorously.

Gideon gave a deep, throaty chuckle, even as he shook his head ruefully. 'Yep, you're my brother, all right!' he acknowledged dryly. 'Mockery in the face of emotion is definitely a family trait,' he explained ruefully.

'Really?' Jonny pursed his lips thoughtfully. 'I wondered where that came from!'

Gideon sobered, frowning slightly. 'So what do we do now? I accept that you're my brother.' It would be impossible to deny it when faced with such physical evidence as the clear similarities between Jonny and himself! And he doubted Edgar, or even Susan Delaney, had any reason to claim the relationship between them if it wasn't the truth.

Even Susan Delaney...!

There lay a very serious problem in discovering he had a younger brother. A brother, he freely acknowledged to himself, he would probably, in time, grow to love and admire. But he actively hated the woman who was Johnny's—and Madison's—mother!

'But you aren't so sure about accepting my mother,' Jonny softly finished for him, having stood and watched the different emotions flickering across Gideon's face.

His mouth tightened. He was very sure about his feelings concerning Susan Delaney, and the fact that she was the mother of his brother didn't change that.

'How about my sister?'

Gideon looked up sharply, finding himself looking into a pair of grey eyes that were as sharply intelligent as his own. 'Madison?' he questioned with deliberate lightness. 'What about her?'

Jonny shrugged, his expression mild. 'You tell me.'

He turned away. 'There's nothing to tell. Madison is contracted to star in the film I'm in the process of directing.'

'Are you going to let her fulfil that contract? You gave the impression earlier that you wished her as far away from here—and you—as possible,' Jonny pointed out softly.

Gideon drew in a deep breath. What was he going to do about Madison?

He'd asked himself that question once before, on the day of the film première, in fact, and his answer then had been that what he wanted to do was make love to her until neither of them could think straight! But that was no longer even an option…!

He turned away. 'I believe you brought me out here to tell me about my father—and your mother,' he reminded his brother hardly.

For a moment Jonny looked as if he wasn't going to be sidetracked from pursuing the subject of Madison, and then he gave a shrug of acceptance that the subject of their father and his mother was the reason they had come out here to talk. 'Don't interrupt until I've finished, hmm?' he said ruefully. 'I'm aware that jumping in with both feet—or both fists—is also a family trait!' He easily referred to the physical violence they had both resorted to at the hospital earlier.

During the last month, it seemed, Gideon had begun to lose all the inhibitions he had built up over a lifetime. He didn't drink alcohol, and yet last night he'd done exactly that, if only a sip. He refused ever to become so angry that he resorted to the violence that had possessed his father that last year of his life, and yet he knew he had intended hitting Jonny at the hospital earlier, and on Saturday night he *had* hit the man who was attempting to mug him, although he'd accepted the latter was a question of self-defence. And, lastly, he had sworn never to fall in love—

'Go ahead,' he invited Jonathan tightly. 'All I can promise is that I'll try not to interrupt,' he added self-derisively.

That promise became incredibly difficult to keep as Jonathan talked, the things Gideon was told about what had happened thirty years ago at such variance with what he had always believed!

Jonny explained that his mother, although only in her early twenties, had already been a star in her own right when she had met John Byrne, who was starring opposite her in one of his films.

History repeating itself…?

No way! Gideon decided fiercely as Jonny continued to talk of the past.

His father had become besotted with the actress; the fact that she rebuffed all of his advances had made no difference to his feelings. But Susan Delaney was a Catholic, and as such refused to become involved with a married man.

So his father had stopped being married, had believed that once he was free the actress would return the love he had for her. But because of her religion Susan didn't believe in divorce either; in her eyes John Byrne was still a married man. And he always would be.

That was when John Byrne's love had become obsessive—sending Susan flowers daily, following her around, causing scenes if she should talk to another man for too long, just generally making her life impossible.

The saddest thing of all, Jonny claimed, was that his mother was attracted to the actor, and in other circumstances she would have been happy to be with him; she'd been in love with him too...!

Gideon had heard enough. 'I don't believe any of this!' he burst out contemptuously. 'Your mother has told you what she thinks you should hear, given you a whiter-than-white account of her own involvement in what happened—'

'No, Gideon, she hasn't,' Jonny assured him harshly. 'Edgar knows the truth too; you can ask him—'

'He's biased,' Gideon dismissed disgustedly. 'He was obviously in love with your mother all those years ago too!' Was. Because, after what Claire had told him of her involvement with Edgar, Gideon believed his assistant would soon marry the older man...

'Yes, he was.' Jonny gave a smile of affection. 'But then she was, and still is, very beautiful. Madison looks very like her, don't you think...?' He quirked questioning eyebrows.

Gideon glared at him. 'Very,' he confirmed tautly, refusing to be drawn any further than that on any comments concerning Madison. 'Unfortunately,' he added tightly.

Jonny sighed. 'Now who's being biased?' He shook his head. 'Like Madison, my mother is one of the nicest, warmest women you are ever likely to meet—I know you don't want to hear that, that you don't ever want to believe it, but I'm telling you it's a fact.'

'She had an affair with a married man,' Gideon pointed out scathingly.

'No, she didn't.' Jonny met his gaze, holding it steadily. 'I told you, she loved him, and loving someone, even when you personally believe it to be wrong, makes it incredibly difficult to keep saying no—'

'Your existence shows that thirty years ago she must have changed her mind at some stage and said yes!' Gideon scorned.

Jonny sighed as he seemed to read his thoughts. 'My mother freely admits she made a mistake, that she foolishly, briefly, allowed her heart to rule her head. But only the once, Gideon,' he added softly.

His mouth twisted. 'Once is all it takes—you are evidence of that!'

Jonny sighed, shaking his head. 'I realise why you hate my mother, Gideon. I know you believe she deliberately took your father away from you, and your mother. What I'm trying to tell you is that she gave him no encouragement; that yes, briefly, many months after he'd already left your mother, she made a mistake—but surely the fact that she found herself pregnant and unmarried was punishment enough for that mistake?'

'She could have married my father,' he insisted 'From what you've said, he was desperate for her to do so!'

But Gideon was aware that his anger had lost some of its fierceness. Because he wanted to believe it? Because— No! He wasn't going to think of that; wasn't going to think of Madison!

Jonny shook his head again. 'Our father died the night my mother became pregnant. She'd told him it couldn't— mustn't—ever happen again. He was angry when he left her, and—she never saw him alive again.'

'So she tricked Malcolm McGuire into marrying her,' Gideon said disgustedly. 'It must have been a shock to him when his "son" was born bearing no facial resemblance to him, and with dark hair!'

'You know, Gideon,' Jonny said mildly, 'I decided long ago that bitterness only destroys the person who carries it around with them. Contrary to what you want to believe, my mother told Malcolm the truth from the first.' He looked defiantly at Gideon. 'The two of them had been seeing each other before our father came on the scene, and when my mother told Malcolm of her pregnancy he told her that he loved her anyway, and asked her to marry him. But I can assure you that never, at any time, did my mother try to pass me off as Malcolm's child. He just happened to love her enough to want her in his life, even carrying another man's child. Look at my name, Gideon,' he continued forcefully. 'I was named after my real father. With Malcolm's full consent.'

Gideon shook his head, his mouth tight. 'I'm not sure I could have done what he obviously did; Malcolm must be one hell of a man!' And he had the feeling he would like the chance to meet him one day...

'He is,' Jonny assured him. 'And, despite its shaky beginning, the marriage has been a good one, too. The two of them are very happy together, and they've made a happy home for Madison and myself.'

Madison again!

'I'm sure Edgar would rather your mother had married him,' he muttered caustically.

'As a matter of fact he did ask her,' Jonny drawled. 'But she decided against it.'

'She was a popular lady,' Gideon scorned.

'Am I getting to you, Gideon?' Jonny taunted, raising mocking brows. '"Mockery in the face of emotion"...?' he reminded him knowingly.

Gideon grinned ruefully. 'You know, I always thought it was lonely being an only child, but now I'm beginning to wonder if it didn't have its advantages...!'

Jonny chuckled softly. 'I'm going back inside now, Gideon.' He lightly touched Gideon's arm. 'I think you need a few minutes to yourself, if only to think about what I've just said.'

He needed more than just a few minutes; the things Jonny had told him, if he were to accept them as the truth, turned everything he had ever believed about the past upside down. They also gave a different view of Susan Delaney... What he had to decide now was whether he could accept her as a woman who'd had no real involvement in breaking up Gideon's family, but who had finally succumbed to the love she felt for Gideon's father. And had to live with that mistake for the rest of her life.

Or was it all just too much to take on board...?

'Oh, and Gideon...' Johnny turned, pausing on his walk back to the house.

Gideon looked at him, frowning. 'Yes?' he prompted warily.

'While you're out here, big bro, you might also want to take a little time to think of what you're going to do about Madison,' the younger man suggested softly, before calmly continuing his walk towards the house.

Gideon watched him go, shaken by the term 'big bro', but knowing he already liked the younger man. He reminded him of himself. But a Gideon that hadn't been affected by his parents' broken marriage. Although Jonny had known more than his share of heartache—he must have been shocked to learn of his true parentage, no matter how he might claim it hadn't really seemed that important to him.

But then, maybe it hadn't. Jonny had obviously grown up completely confident in the love of both his parents. And that of his younger sister.

Madison...!

Back to that same haunting question: what was he, Gideon, going to *do* about Madison?

CHAPTER TWELVE

MADISON felt herself tense nervously as she heard the front door to the house open and then softly close again. Her mother and Edgar had just told her exactly the same as Jonny claimed he had explained to Gideon—how much more upsetting it must have been for Gideon than it was for her!

All she felt, at being told the truth about the past, was love for her mother, great admiration for her father, and aching love for Gideon. Because he'd had the whole fabric of his life turned upside down!

And all of that on top of learning that Claire, the woman he loved, was actually involved with Edgar!

She turned to look at Gideon as she sensed him standing in the open doorway. The other three, at Johnny's suggestion, had gone upstairs to the empty bedrooms, to freshen up after their journey. Actually, Madison believed the real reason for that was so that Gideon didn't have to be confronted by her mother and Edgar as soon as he came back into the house, but she outwardly accepted the excuse that had been given to her.

'Hi.' She greeted Gideon warily.

'Hi.' He nodded abruptly, moving into the room, his hands thrust into his trouser pockets.

Madison continued to watch him with apprehensive eyes as he strolled around, apparently looking at the few ornaments that adorned the room. But Madison was sure he had no real interest in the inexpensive trinkets.

She moistened her lips nervously; if this silence was allowed to continue for too long, it would become unbearable—and unbreakable! 'I'm so sorry,' she told him huskily.

Gideon frowned and turned to her. 'What the hell are you sorry for?' he demanded.

She swallowed hard. 'My mother and Edgar told me what happened thirty years ago too, and—'

'Exactly,' he cut in scornfully. 'Thirty years ago! You weren't even born, Madison,' he dismissed impatiently.

No, she wasn't. And if things had turned out differently, if her mother had married John Byrne, or even Edgar, then she might never have been born...! As it was, it appeared that her brother was also Gideon's brother. And, from the little Jonny had said to them when he came back, she didn't think there was too much chance of her never seeing Gideon again, because it seemed he and Jonny were going to get to know each other. Each time she saw Gideon as Jonny's brother she would know the pain of losing the man she loved all over again!

'Madison, it's all right.' Gideon cut in on her tortured thoughts, frowning across at her. 'It's been a shock, but— Once I get used to the idea, I think I'm going to like having a younger brother,' he admitted gruffly.

She was glad, so very glad; Gideon deserved to have a family of his own. But where did that leave her? What did that make her? The fact that Gideon was Jonny's half-brother didn't mean she was related to Gideon in any way, and yet he would be a part of her family, nonetheless.

'And my mother...?' she prompted warily.

He drew in a deep breath. 'That's going to take me a little more time to come to terms with, but— I'll get there, Madison,' he assured her confidently.

And what about her? What about the movie? What happened *now*?

'You look very like her,' Gideon bit out abruptly.

And he despised her for it! She did look like her mother,

very much so from the photographs she had seen of her when she was younger. Which was why, when Madison had decided to go into acting herself, she'd done so under her own name of McGuire. She'd wanted to succeed or fail on her own merit, and not on the back of her mother's undoubted fame.

Until Edgar's interference, she'd been attempting to do just that. Maybe not too successfully, but at least her achievements so far had been her own. Which was why it had angered her so much to learn of Edgar's interference over the part offered to her in Gideon's movie.

She turned away. 'You'll naturally want to recast the role of Rosemary—'

'What?' Gideon exclaimed sharply. 'After all the hassle I've had with you so far? No way! You signed a contract, you'll damn well keep to it!'

'But—'

'There are no buts, Madison,' he told her grimly. 'Admittedly, I would rather your mother were anyone other than Susan Delaney. But who knows?' he shrugged. 'Maybe it will turn out to be a bonus in the end!'

Once again, it was 'work as usual' with Gideon! Nothing, and no one, must be allowed to interfere with that. And his implication seemed to be that her mother's identity would do to pull out of a hat at some moment that would suit him, and the publicity for his movie!

Her mouth tightened. 'My mother and Jonny intend returning to the States in the next day or so.'

'You won't be going with them,' he warned her gratingly.

Madison felt an angry flush colour her cheeks. 'This situation is impossible now, Gideon—'

'Why?'

She couldn't quite meet the challenge in that gaze. Because she couldn't even begin to explain just how impossible this situation was without admitting that she had fallen in love with him!

She swallowed hard. 'Things have changed, Gideon—'

'In what way?' he prompted tensely.

'In every way!' she insisted emotionally. 'You've met my mother, know who she is now. You've been made aware that Jonny is your brother. And—and Edgar and Claire appear to be in love with each other!' She saved the worst until last.

Because surely Claire's love for the other man, loving her as Gideon did himself, must have some effect on him?

He nodded grimly. 'To such an extent that it seems the two of them are going to be married.'

And what was he going to do about that? Or was he still so determined never to admit to loving anyone that he would let the woman he loved just walk away with another man?

'And that doesn't bother you?' Madison frowned.

'It's inconvenient—'

'Inconvenient!' she repeated disgustedly.

Gideon nodded, his mouth twisting derisively. 'It seems Edgar isn't too keen on her traveling the world with me once the two of them are married, and she'll be getting a job a little closer to home.' He shrugged. 'I can see the sense in that.'

'You can?' Madison gave him a disbelieving look.

'Of course. I'm not sure I would be too keen on my own wife going off round the world with another man, either. Even if it was work,' he added grimly.

'You don't have a wife!' Madison muttered frustratedly. She couldn't believe he was really taking this as calmly as he appeared to be!

'True,' he acknowledged. 'But if I did have one I would feel exactly the same way as Edgar does where Claire is concerned.' He shook his head. 'Long-distance marriages don't work; my parents' divorce is evidence of that. Who knows? Maybe if my father hadn't been away so often working the two of them might never have split up. Edgar is just ensuring the same mistake doesn't happen in his marriage to Claire. Hell, he's waited long enough for the right woman; he isn't going to make any mistakes now!' he added affectionately.

Once again Madison had the feeling that there was something not quite right here. Gideon loved Claire himself— didn't he? If he didn't, why had he been so affected when they had visited Claire in hospital last night? Had she missed something?

She shook her head. 'I don't understand you. You're going to let her go, just like that?'

'What choice do I have? I can hardly stop her getting married; she's a big girl, more than capable of making her own decisions. Besides,' he added thoughtfully, 'I think they'll actually be happy together.'

So did Madison. Both Claire and Edgar had obviously waited until they found the right person before even contemplating marriage, and so Madison knew it wasn't a decision they had come to lightly. But, nevertheless…!

'But you love Claire!' she pointed out frustratedly.

'Well, of course I do; she's always— Wait a minute…' Gideon looked at her searchingly. 'When you say I love Claire, do you mean…?'

'I mean as in love and marriage!' Madison confirmed agitatedly. 'Gideon, I saw how upset you were when we went to the hospital last night—'

'Well, of course I was upset,' he snapped impatiently. 'Claire had been involved in a car accident!'

'Exactly.' Madison pounced. 'Gideon, don't you think it's time you stopped living behind the barrier you've erected around your emotions? Because if you don't you're going to lose the woman you love to someone else!'

His face lost all expression, but his eyes glittered keenly. 'It's serious, then?' he muttered grimly.

'Haven't I just been telling you so?' Madison's voice rose incredulously.

Gideon shook his head, his expression one of puzzlement now. 'I'm not absolutely sure what you've been talking about! A minute ago we were talking about Claire and Edgar, and some mistaken idea that I'm in love with Claire myself, and now we seem to have moved on to Simon Cauley—'

'Simon?' she repeated dazedly. 'I never mentioned Simon! I—'

'Not by name, perhaps,' Gideon conceded harshly. 'But the implication was there.'

Madison stared at him. What implication? She hadn't even given Simon a thought over the last couple of days—why should she? He was a friend, nothing more—and she certainly couldn't see where he came into this now!

'Could we go back a few steps in the conversation?' She frowned her bemusement. 'You see, I don't understand where Simon came into this at all…! I was trying to jolt you out of this emotional fortress you seem to have built around yourself, explaining to you that you were going to lose Claire if you didn't do something about it, and all of a sudden the subject had changed to Simon—' She broke off abruptly, stunned as she replayed their conversation in her mind. 'Gideon…?' She looked across at him uncertainly.

She'd warned Gideon that he was in danger of losing the woman he loved to another man—and he had been the one to start talking about Simon Cauley! Did that mean—?

'Madison.' Gideon had moved across the room, standing only inches away from her now, looking down at her with dark grey eyes as he reached out to grasp her arms. 'I have no idea how you got the impression I'm in love with

Claire.' He shook his head dazedly. 'I do love her, but I'm not *in* love with her. And, as I'm learning only too well, there's a vast difference between the two,' he added self-derisively. 'And the answer to your question of a few minutes ago is I'm not going to just sit back and let another man walk away with the woman I love because of some damned barrier I have around my emotions!' he muttered grimly. 'Be it Simon Cauley, or the man you were involved with before you came to London in need of TLC!' he added with a return of some of his old arrogance.

Gideon was in love with her! When—? How—? What—?

His hands tightened on her arms as he shook her slightly. 'For obvious reasons, I've always made it a rule never to become involved with anyone I work with, but I'm giving you fair notice; you're contracted to work with me for at least the next eight months—and I'm going to use every minute of that time to try and persuade you into loving me in return!'

Unbelievable!

Incredible!

Amazing!

Wonderful…!

Madison shook her head. 'I don't need any convincing, Gideon.' She laughed huskily, putting her hands on his shoulders as she gazed up into his face. 'I already love you!' she explained happily as he looked down at her blankly. 'And I've been breaking my heart the last twenty-four hours imagining you were in love with Claire!' she admitted emotionally.

Gideon's arms moved about her like steel bands as he crushed her to him. 'I think you have an over-active imagination, young lady,' he groaned. 'I was upset last night at the hospital because I couldn't stand to see you in tears, not because I am, or ever have been, in love with Claire!'

Madison's face was buried in the warmth of his chest as she clung to him. 'And I'm not in love with Simon, either; he's an old schoolfriend of Jonny's, that's all. And as for Gerry—'

'The man who gave you reason to need TLC?' Gideon looked down at her.

She met his gaze confidently. 'I can't even remember what he looks like!' And it was true. All other men had faded into insignificance since meeting and falling in love with Gideon!

'Don't even try,' Gideon warned possessively. 'Now kiss me, woman—before I go quietly out of my mind!' he groaned throatily.

She was quite happy to comply with his request. In fact, more than happy, the two of them losing themselves in the passion that was never far away when they were together. Gideon loved her. It was more, much more than she had ever hoped for.

'Madi— Oh!'

Madison felt Gideon tense, giving him a searching look before turning slowly to face her mother as she stood uncertainly in the doorway. The fact that Madison was held closely in Gideon's arms obviously told its own story.

But Madison's main worry was how Gideon, after talking to Jonny, was going to react to her mother...

Gideon didn't know how to react as he looked at Susan Delaney. He knew more about the past now, and as such understood things a bit better, but it was difficult to restrain his old antagonism.

And then he looked down at Madison, the woman he loved, and who—miraculously!—loved him in return, aware of the apprehension in her gaze as she looked from one to the other of them. Susan Delaney was her mother, and Madison obviously loved her very much. Gideon certainly had no right to ever ask her to choose between her family and himself. Especially as part of that family— Jonny—was already his own!

He squeezed Madison's arm reassuringly before turning to walk towards Susan Delaney. 'Mrs. McGuire,' he greeted warmly, holding out his hand. 'I'm sorry we weren't formally introduced earlier. I'm Gideon Byrne.'

The actress looked uncertain for a moment, and then she reached out and put the slenderness of her own hand into his much larger one. 'Am I to take it, from the scene I just interrupted, that my daughter's name is soon to be Byrne too?' Susan Delaney prompted huskily.

Gideon grinned, knowing that a milestone had been passed. He wasn't naive; he knew that he and Madison's mother weren't going to become at ease with each other overnight, but at least they had made a start. 'I haven't actually had a chance to ask her yet…but I'm hoping so, yes.' He turned to look warily at Madison.

Loving him was one thing, but hoping Madison would marry him was something else…!

It hadn't taken him long after Jonny's return to the house to know exactly what he wanted 'to do about Madison', and he knew that nothing less than marriage, the promise of for ever, would do!

It was a complete about-face from his previous attitude towards love and marriage, he knew that, but the truth of the matter was, the thought of Madison as his wife made him shake with longing…!

Madison moved gracefully to his side, slipping her hand confidently into his. 'I think Madison Byrne sounds just right,' she assured him huskily, her love for him shining in emerald-bright eyes as she smiled up at him.

'Can I take that as a yes?' Gideon murmured breathlessly.

'I'll leave you two alone to talk.' Susan Delaney squeezed his arm before turning to go back upstairs.

Gideon turned Madison easily back into his arms. 'I love you very much, Madison McGuire, and you would make me the happiest man in the world if you would become my wife.' There. He had said the words he had thought he would never say to any woman.

But the thought of being without Madison ever again was totally unacceptable to him. He loved her as he had never thought he would love any woman. And he desperately wanted her to be his wife, to share his life, for always.

'Gladly, Gideon,' she accepted emotionally. 'Because I love you very much too.'

'Let's make it soon, Madison,' he groaned as he held her closely to him once again.

'As soon as you like,' she agreed huskily.

'In that case,' he laughed down at her, 'I suggest your mother and Jonny stay right here, and we get your father to come over too; that way we can be married in a matter of days!'

'Yes, please, Gideon,' Madison said breathlessly.

He'd never realised how loving someone could change your life, giving a different perspective on everything. And having that someone love you in return was the most marvellous feeling in the world.

He was determined that with Madison and himself it would always be that way...

EPILOGUE

EDGAR knew he hadn't felt this nervous since the day he and Claire had married six months ago. Although that had turned out to be the best thing he'd ever done in his life, so hopefully the Oscars award ceremony would turn out just as successfully for *Rosemary*!

There was no doubting the fact that the film had taken the box offices of the world by storm. The last four months had been full of newspaper and magazine articles about Madison and Gideon, the fact that the two of them turned out to have been married to each other for the last ten months only adding to the public interest *Rosemary* had generated.

They were all seated together as they waited for the results to be read out throughout the evening: Madison and Gideon, Susan and Malcolm, Jonny, and Claire and himself. It was amazing how much of a family they had all become over the last year, the painful memories of the past having been superseded by the much happier ones of the present.

'We just have to find Jonny a wife, and we can all be happy,' he murmured to Claire during a lull in the proceedings.

His wife turned to give him a teasing smile, linking her arm in his. 'You old romantic, you.' She hugged his arm affectionately. 'But I should leave Jonny to find his own wife.'

'But our last effort turned out so well.' He nodded in the direction of Madison and Gideon, the happiness they shared together shining out of them.

'All the more reason to quit while you're ahead,' Claire advised practically.

She was probably right, although it seemed a shame that Jonathan was still on his own. Having at last tried the marital state, Edgar could only recommend it.

Although all thought of that went out of his head as the results of the Oscars began to be announced. Three hours later they all had ample reason for the celebratory dinner Edgar had already arranged for them; *Rosemary* had won Best film, Gideon had won Best Director and Best Screenplay, and Madison had won Best Actress!

'Tonight couldn't possibly be improved upon!' Edgar toasted as they sat in the restaurant an hour later, raising his champagne glass.

'Oh, we think it could,' Gideon murmured emotionally, his arm about Madison's shoulders as he smiled down at her with open love and pride. 'Madison and I are expecting a baby in five months!'

The next few minutes were taken up with ecstatic reactions to the news, Madison and Gideon obviously euphoric over the pregnancy.

'Well, that makes you two grandparents.' Edgar nodded at Susan and Malcolm. 'But, as Madison's godfather, what does it make me?' He arched questioning brows.

'Er—actually…' Claire spoke slowly. 'It makes you a father too!'

Edgar turned to look at her, uncomprehending, the sound of the laughter of the others at the table going completely over his head as Claire's meaning became clear to him.

A *father*? *He* was going to be a father!

'I'm sixty-three years old, for goodness' sake,' he finally gasped.

'But obviously not past it, Edgar,' Gideon drawled mockingly.

'Don't get smart, Gideon.' Edgar glared at him. 'I don't know anything about babies,' he told Claire worriedly.

'Don't worry about it, darling.' Claire patted his hand soothingly. 'It won't be here for another seven months, and by that time Madison and Gideon will be old hands at parenthood, and can give us some tips.'

Tips? He was going to need more than tips! A *baby*...!

A son. A little boy of his own. Or maybe a daughter. As beautiful as her mother. Hell, he didn't care what it was; it would be their child. Emotion such as he had never known before swept over him as he began to grin happily.

Who ever would have thought a year go that they would all be sitting here happily together like this? He certainly hadn't.

But he had no complaints, no complaints at all. And as he looked around the table at all the other smiling faces he didn't think any of them had any, either...

MILLS & BOON®

Makes any time special

Copyright © Harlequin Enterprises Limited 1997
All rights reserved

Enjoy a romantic novel from Mills & Boon®

Presents...™   *Enchanted™*   TEMPTATION®

Historical Romance™   ⅃ **MEDICAL ROMANCE®**

MILLS & BOON®

Presents...™

THE UNEXPECTED HUSBAND *by Lindsay Armstrong*

Lydia was thrilled by her assignment on an Australian cattle station—until she came face to face with tough, sexy Joe Jordan on her first day. Joe made it clear that he wanted to marry her! But did he just want a convenient wife?

A SUSPICIOUS PROPOSAL *by Helen Brooks*

Millionaire business man Xavier Grey seemed intent on pursuing Essie. And he was used to getting what he wanted! But when he proposed, was it an affair or marriage he had in mind…and could Essie trust him?

THE SURROGATE MOTHER *by Lilian Darcy*

After her cousin's death, surrogate mother Julie was suddenly the *only* mother for the baby she was carrying. But, when the baby's father, Tom Callahan, insisted on marriage, Julie feared he'd never see her as anything but a surrogate—wife, mother or lover…

CONTRACT BRIDEGROOM *by Sandra Field*

Celia wanted to grant her dying father's wish to see her 'happily married', so she was paying Jethro Lathem to be her temporary husband. Then she discovered Jethro was a multimillionaire! Why on earth had he agreed to marry her? Moreover, their 'no sex' agreement was proving to be a nightmare—for both of them!

Available from 7th July 2000

Available at most branches of WH Smith, Tesco, Martins, Borders, Easons, Volume One/James Thin and most good paperback bookshops

0006/01a

MILLS & BOON®

Presents...™

THE COZAKIS BRIDE *by Lynne Graham*

Olivia had no choice: her mother urgently needed expensive medical treatment, so she'd have to beg Nik Cozakis to marry her. Nik agreed, but only if Olivia bore him a son…

ROMANO'S REVENGE *by Sandra Marton*

When Joe's new cook turned out to be blonde, beautiful—and useless in the kitchen—he knew it was the work of his matchmaking grandmother. So he decided to add posing as his fiancée to Lucinda's list of duties. Lucinda could cope with a pretend engagement—but she drew the line at sharing Joe's bed!

THE MILLIONAIRE'S VIRGIN *by Anne Mather*

Nikolas has obviously not forgiven Paige for walking out on him four years ago. So why has he offered her a job on his Greek island for the summer? And what exactly will he be expecting from her?

THE PLAYBOY'S PROPOSITION *by Miranda Lee*

Tyler Garrison was impossibly handsome, and heir to a fortune. So Michele was touched by his plan to escort her to her ex-boyfriend's wedding as her pretend lover. But she was shocked when he proposed they become lovers for real—what was his motive?

Available from 7th July 2000

Available at most branches of WH Smith, Tesco, Martins, Borders, Easons, Volume One/James Thin and most good paperback bookshops

0006/01b

Emma Darcy brings you...

Kings of the

OUTBACK

Meet the Kings, three brothers with three very different lifestyles, all living in the outback of Australia. Join the Kings of the Outback in their search for soulmates.

The Playboy King's Wife

4th August

The Pleasure King's Bride

3rd November

Available at most branches of WH Smith, Tesco,
Martins, Borders, Easons, Volume One/James Thin
and most good paperback bookshops   0005/01/LC02a

FREE

4 BOOKS
AND A SURPRISE GIFT!

We would like to take this opportunity to thank you for reading this Mills & Boon® book by offering you the chance to take FOUR more specially selected titles from the Presents...™ series absolutely FREE! We're also making this offer to introduce you to the benefits of the Reader Service™—

★ FREE home delivery   ★ FREE gifts and competitions
★ FREE monthly Newsletter   ★ Exclusive Reader Service discounts
★ Books available before they're in the shops

Accepting these FREE books and gift places you under no obligation to buy; you may cancel at any time, even after receiving your free shipment. Simply complete your details below and return the entire page to the address below. **You don't even need a stamp!**

YES! Please send me 4 free Presents...™ books and a surprise gift. I understand that unless you hear from me, I will receive 6 superb new titles every month for just £2.40 each, postage and packing free. I am under no obligation to purchase any books and may cancel my subscription at any time. The free books and gift will be mine to keep in any case. POEC

Ms/Mrs/Miss/Mr ....Initials ....
BLOCK CAPITALS PLEASE

Surname ....

Address ....

....

....Postcode ....

Send this whole page to:
UK: FREEPOST CN81, Croydon, CR9 3WZ
EIRE: PO Box 4546, Kilcock, County Kildare (stamp required)

Offer valid in UK and Eire only and not available to current Reader Service subscribers to this series. We reserve the right to refuse an application and applicants must be aged 18 years or over. Only one application per household. Terms and prices subject to change without notice. Offer expires 31st December 2000. As a result of this application, you may receive further offers from Harlequin Mills & Boon Limited and other carefully selected companies. If you would prefer not to share in this opportunity please write to The Data Manager at the address above.

Mills & Boon® is a registered trademark owned by Harlequin Mills & Boon Limited.
Presents...™ is being used as a trademark.

0006/05

MILLS & BOON®

Makes any time special™

By Request

Marriages
by Arrangement

A MARRIAGE HAS BEEN ARRANGED
by Anne Weale

Pierce Sutherland is the only man Holly has ever wanted, but her glamorous blonde stepsister is more his type. So when Pierce proposes a marriage of convenience, can Holly's pride allow her to accept?

TO TAME A PROUD HEART
by Cathy Williams

Francesca Wade is determined to prove her worth to her employer. Yet one night of passion has her out of Oliver Kemp's office and up the aisle—with a man too proud to love her, but too honourable to leave her!

NEVER A BRIDE by Diana Hamilton

Jake Winter was every woman's fantasy—and Claire's husband! But their marriage was a purely business arrangement—so how was Claire to tell Jake she'd fallen in love with him?

**Look out for *Marriages* by Arrangement
in July 2000**

*Available at branches of WH Smith, Tesco, Martins, Borders, Easons,
Volume One/James Thin and most good paperback bookshops*